The Switch Family

A Novel by

CHRISTOPHER J. MOORE

Copyright

Dedication

I dedicate this book to my kids, Jordan, Xavier, and Christiahn. May it become one of your favorites.

Table of Contents

Chapter 1

T he wind was cold in the vast forest of South Carolina. Clouds loomed over the trees and hills. Leaves danced through the forest as the wind kicked up.

The moonlight started to make its move on the night, slicing through the branches deep in the forest. A rabbit frolicked without a care in the world. Suddenly, a young girl ran through the thick underbrush, startling the rabbit. Her clothes were tattered, her legs cut up, and she looked like she had been through hell. She ran desperately through the woods, becoming more terrified with each wild step. She looked to be around sixteen.

She could hear her doom.

A dozen black combat boots pursued her.

"She's over there. I hear her over there!" a man shouted.

"Spread out!" another man yelled.

The girl jumped off a hill and continued to run. "I see her!" yelled a woman with spiked hair and piercings in her face. They continued to give chase. The young girl hurtled a bush. A man in his forties who looked like a hillbilly darted after her.

"I see her," the hillbilly shouted.

"Damn, she's fast," a tattooed man shouted.

The young girl ran as fast as she could until she took a violent spill and fell ten feet. Her head slammed against a tree hard; her eyes rolled around in her head as she lay sprawled on the ground. She gathered her bearings and got up but it was too late. Men and women dressed in black fatigues were right on top of her, guns drawn. She stared up at them, petrified. Gimon, a man with a brazen tattoo of a flame on his neck, stared down at her menacingly. His eyes were piercing gray and extremely intense. He also had an ugly scar on the side of his face.

"Why are you doing this?" the young girl asked.

Gimon took his time before answering, savoring the moment.

"Because you are an abomination," he said in a gruff monotone voice.

"I haven't done anything," she cried out.

"And you won't."

"Who are you?"

"Gimon…"

"Whatever I did, Gimon, I'm sorry. Just let me go. And you'll never see me again."

"I can't do that."

"Why not?" she asked, baffled, her eyes pleading.

He put his gun in his waistband and took out a transmitter that resembled a walkie-talkie. He waved it slowly in front of her. It made a crackling sound and the light on the front changed from yellow to green. "That's why." His eyes narrowed. Gimon stared at her with no remorse as he reached for his gun.

"No. No!" she screamed.

He slowly raised his gun to her face, leaned in, and fired.

Chapter 2

I t was another perfect day in a beach community in San Diego, California. People rode bicycles, skated, and jogged while others shopped and walked their dogs.

Emily, seventeen, beautiful with bright blue eyes and sandy blond hair, ran across the track at her high school and handed Kelly who was the same age a bottle of cold water. Kelly nodded in gratitude but didn't say anything. Her expression was that of someone who was about to go to war. Kelly had smooth skin, like a porcelain doll that had been dipped in dark chocolate. Her hair was pulled back in a ponytail and she was sporting a green and white uniform. She was stunning, and was in great spirits, just like the other girls eager to run. They all stood at the starting line. Kelly gazed at the crowd in the stands cheering them on.

Kelly and the other sprinters slowly knelt in a four-point stance. Kelly focused her dark brown eyes that appeared black on the finish line. She could hear her heart beat louder and louder, speeding up with each second. She tuned everything out. The crowd, the other runners. Everyone. She waited, eyes slowly closing. Then, *bang*.

Kelly took off. She quickly left the other runners behind, jumping the hurtles with perfect form. The others competed for second place as Kelly continued to pull away from the pack.

She crossed the finish line, throwing her hands up in victory. She looked at the time board. She saw *New School Record* flashing in bright lights. She smiled.

Kelly hugged a few of her teammates close to her, then she and a few other girls jogged over to the stands. There was a black family cheering the girls on. Another black girl went to that family in the stands, while Kelly went to her family, which was all white. They hugged Kelly, ecstatic.

Kelly sat in the back of her parent's SUV with her sister Emily. Emily had her hair in a ponytail. She had the same sandy blond hair as her mother and father. And the same piercing blue eyes as her mother, Linda. Her father, Victor, laughed as he drove. Linda sat in the passenger seat, holding his hand. Victor looked at Kelly in the rearview mirror, proud.

"You were so good, baby," Victor said.

"She was awesome," Emily added.

"You are getting so fast," Linda said in awe.

"You the man, baby!" Victor said.

"You mean, the woman," Kelly responded, smiling, knowing how good she was.

"That's right, baby, you tell him," Linda said.

"Yeah yeah, that's what I meant."

"God, it felt good. I mean when I was running, I just felt like I could fly!"

"My sister, future gold medalist," Emily said.

"I am so proud of you," Victor added, wearing a huge smile. Kelly beamed with pride. "Anyone hungry?" The girls lit up.

Christopher J. Moore

They ended up at a seafood restaurant, with a view of the beach behind them.

"Dad, can we go somewhere tropical for our summer vacation?" Kelly asked.

"Yeah, how about Jamaica?" Emily added.

"I can do Jamaica," Linda said with a smile.

"Me too," Kelly said, teasing her dad with the same smile.

"I got a feeling you guys planned this little Jamaican ambush." Linda and the girls all looked at each other, giddy. "See, I knew it."

"Come on dad. Last year we went to Alaska," Kelly said as if it left a bad taste in her mouth.

"I hated Alaska!" Emily said.

"It wasn't that bad," Victor said, amused.

"It was bad. Everything that could go wrong, did," Linda said.

"Hey, why don't we just go somewhere close? Like Palm Springs?" Victor said. Linda looked at him oddly.

"I'm not trying to go to Palm Springs. We can go there anytime," Linda said.

Victor thought for a moment, then sighed.

"Honey, we have to scale back on our spending. I didn't want to say anything, but my contract was canceled nine months ago. We've been living off of our savings." She looked concerned.

"How come you didn't tell me?" Linda asked.

"Because I didn't want you to worry. I figured I'd get a new contract by now and we'd be fine. The trucking business is usually pretty consistent."

"But you haven't got another contract?"

"No. Not yet. But I will."

"So what does that mean? No Jamaica?" Emily asked. Kelly looked disappointed. Linda and Victor looked at the girls as if they had no concept of money.

"Let's just focus on today. I don't want to talk about finances," Victor said, feeling a little stressed.

"Well I do," Linda said. Victor and Linda looked at the girls.

"We know, we know," the girls said without missing a beat. The two got up.

"Restroom," Kelly said.

"Sure," Emily said as they headed to the back of the restaurant.

"Victor, how could you not tell me this? Are we broke?"

"No, we're not broke. We're just financially challenged," he said, attempting to lighten the tension.

She gave a sarcastic smile.

"That sounds broke to me. When were you going to tell me? I could have gotten a job."

"Babe, I don't want you to work."

"Listen. I know you like being the man and all. But this is a different time. If we can swing it, fine, but if we can't, I have to get a job."

"I hear you. I just didn't think that it would take this long. I have another contract I think is coming, so we're gonna be fine."

"Coming when?"

"Two, three months."

"Three months?"

"Yeah. More like four months," he said with a smile. She gave him a stern look. "Four months," he reiterated, biting his bottom lip. "Five months tops." She sighed, feeling the sting of it.

"If you say so."

"I say so. Now, can we enjoy our meal?"

"I don't know. Can we afford it?"

"No, that's why I left the car unlocked so we can run out of here when we're done. So make sure your shoelaces are tied up tight."

"Ha ha."

"We're fine," he said with a smile.

"Okay," Linda said throwing her hands up. She saw the girls standing over by the restroom waiting to come back. Linda waved them over without even looking at them. The girls quickly headed over, eager to get back to their food.

"Great, you guys settled things, 'cause I'm starving," Kelly said as she started to dig in.

"Who you tellin'?" Emily added. The girls continued to eat.

"Yeah yeah," Victor said, amused by the girls. "Like I was saying, we'll go to Jamaica next summer for sure. I promise."

"I don't know why you guys have to act so secret about money. If we got it, we got it; if we don't, we don't," Kelly said.

"I think we should just max out some credit cards and go," Emily said.

"That's a great idea," Kelly said, giving her a high-five.

"You kids have it too easy. When I was a kid, summer vacation was just driving down by the lake, an hour away. None of this Jamaica, Alaska, Spain stuff," Victor said.

"Please don't start telling us how you had to walk ten miles to school every day," Emily said.

"And your parents were so poor, you hardly ate," Kelly added.

"We were," Victor said. Linda gave Victor a stop exaggerating look. "Okay, maybe not that poor."

"Can we change the subject?" Linda said, trying to enjoy her food.

"Now, Spain was fun. That had to be the best trip we ever had," Kelly said, in awe of Spain and the culture there.

"Yeah, Spain was the bomb," Emily added.

"Bomb? Why do you kids talk like that?" Victor asked.

"Dad, you're just old," Kelly said with a smirk.

"Who you calling old? I'm hip."

The girls laughed at their father.

"The fact that you said hip is proof you're not," Emily said, shaking her head.

"I don't need this. Hurry up and finish your food so we can go," Victor said, pretending to be offended. The girls, including Linda, laughed.

The family rode in their SUV with the windows down, enjoying the beautiful sunny weather.

"This might be the best day of my life. I actually won the state championship," Kelly said feeling triumphant. Emily hugged Kelly.

"But you still can't beat me," Victor said.

"Yeah, right. We can pull over now and race," Kelly said, confident in her ability.

"Let's do it," Victor said.

"I'm ready," she said with a smile. Kelly unfastened her seatbelt. Victor quickly unfastened his, accepting the challenge.

"Will you two put your seatbelts back on?" Linda said.

"Shoot, I still got the wheels... but because it's your day, I don't want to mess it up for you by smoking you... I'll concede," Victor said.

"Thanks, daddy," Kelly said, rolling her eyes. She knew her father would not have stood a chance. Kelly hugged her father from behind. They laughed.

"You guys are silly," Linda said.

"Aw, that's so sweet," Emily added with a smile.

"Yeah, that's sweet. Now both of you put on your seatbelts," Linda said for the last time.

A kid on a skateboard jumped off of the curb, right in front of the SUV.

Victor's eyes were down trying to buckle up his seatbelt. "Victor!" Linda screamed. Victor's eyes shot up and saw the kid. He swerved hard, just missing him. The truck flew on to the opposite side of the street. Cars veered out of the way, just missing them. Their SUV flipped over several times and hit a car driving by. Glass shattered from the impact. Emily and Linda's bodies lunged forward, their seatbelts keeping them from going any farther. However, Victor and Kelly both flew through their side windows.

Their bodies flew in an almost dream-like state, with nothing but a cinder block wall in their future, and the afterlife for both of them. Linda's eyes focused, seeing what was to come for both of them. Her eyes went wider than normal and her pupils dilated.

Just as they were about to meet their fates, Linda's hand shot out toward them, slowing Kelly and Victor down in midair.

Regular speed resumed and Linda caught Kelly just before she hit the wall, making them tumble to the ground hard. They both looked at each other stunned and shook up. Kelly looked wild-eyed while Linda looked at Victor's limp body on the sidewalk.

Kelly's eyes followed her mother's line of sight and saw her father dead on the ground, body twisted and bloody. Kelly was frozen, as tears rolled down her cheeks.

The truck had landed on its tires with only Emily still in it, still buckled up and delirious. The mangled SUV smoked from under the hood. Emily's eyes slowly opened as she gathered her bearings. She saw her sister wrapped in her mother's arms laying on the sidewalk. Then she saw her father. Emily let out a horrifying, heart-wrenching scream.

The Paterson family stood among a group of grieving people dressed in black. Linda and Emily stood there stoic, tears in their eyes. Kelly was more emotional, sobbing uncontrollably. Linda and Emily tried to comfort Kelly as Victor's casket descended into the ground.

The repast was at the Paterson family home. People ate food and respectfully shared memories of Victor, saying what a standup guy he was. Kelly and Emily watched from afar as random people gave their mother their condolences.

The girls wondered who most of these people were; some were obviously people who had worked with their father, but the rest, they had no idea.

Chapter 3

M onths later Linda sat in bed going over some bills. Phone bill, light bill, mortgage, all overdue. She took a hit financially with the funeral arrangements and having to pay off their company's debts. So the little bit of life insurance they did receive, it was gone in no time.

Kelly peeked her head inside the room. "Hey, Mom."

"Hey," Linda replied.

Kelly entered the room and climbed in bed with her.

"What's up?" Linda said as she continued to look over her bills and paperwork.

"Mom, are we going to be okay?"

"What do you mean?"

"Money wise," Kelly said, looking at all of the bills spread out on the bed.

"Of course we are."

"Mom," Kelly said, with a nod to the bills.

"I don't know, Kelly," Linda said, rubbing the stress off her face.

"Are you a little scared?"

"A little. But I still feel really blessed."

Kelly obviously had something on her mind but hesitated talking about it. Then she said what had been on her mind since the accident.

"Speaking of blessed, what are the odds of me being thrown into you, and us landing… safely on the ground." Linda thought for a moment.

"One in a million. Hey, but people win the lottery every day, don't they?" Linda said. Kelly thought about her answer.

"True. But you had on your seat—"

"I guess we were lucky I took off my seatbelt, too."

"But you didn't."

"Of course I did," Linda replied.

"Mom," she said knowingly.

"I took it off and was about to jump in that back seat, and buckle you up myself." Kelly thought for a moment, not sure about anything anymore.

Their eyes both went up, hearing Emily's key opening the front door.

They both sighed, thinking about their family's predicament. Kelly couldn't believe their lives had been changed forever so drastically, all because of one kid on a skateboard and the unbuckling of two seatbelts.

"Mom, I miss daddy so much."

"I do, too. But we're going to regroup, get back on our feet and move forward. Your dad would want that."

"Can we afford to stay here?"

"No. But things will work themselves out, one way or another."

"I just…" Kelly's eyes welled up and she hugged her mother.

"Sweetie…"

"I feel like it was my fault. I should have never taken my seatbelt off."

Linda's eyes welled up as well.

"It wasn't your fault. It was just a freak accident."

Emily, dressed in a pretty skirt, face fully made up peeked her head inside. "Okay, what is it now?" She asked, seeing their flushed faces.

"Nothing," Linda said.

"You guys look like you've been crying."

"So?" Kelly said.

Suddenly a sadness came over Emily's face, too. "Well, I wanna cry," she said.

"Come on sweetie, you can come cry, too," Linda said, waving her over.

Emily's eyes welled up and she got in bed with her mother and sister. Linda put her arms around her girls. They lay in bed all hugged up, not saying a word, covered in a blanket of bills.

Then a whimper, then tears…

Kelly and Emily strolled down a street in their neighborhood, each holding a couple grocery bags.

"I'm kind of worried about mom," Emily said, in deep thought.

"She seems to be doing okay."

"I don't think she's dealing with it."

"She is, just in her own way," Kelly said. She thought for a moment. "I had no idea they were having money problems."

"Well, we're going to have to move. The question is where. And here we were stressing dad out about a vacation," Emily said, feeling like a spoiled brat. They looked at each other, guilt ridden.

"I don't care where we move to. I just want to get out of that house. Every time I step in there I think of daddy," Kelly said.

"Me, too," Emily replied. They continued down the street.

"It's a pretty day," Kelly said as she watched a bird soar through the sky, swoop low, then glide to a telephone wire and land on it with ease.

"Yeah, it is."

"I feel like running," Kelly said, stretching her neck side to side.

"Girl, you always feel like running. You're addicted to running."

"You're probably right. I just suddenly feel inspired. Like I wanna fly."

"Race you home!" Emily said. She knocked a bag out of Kelly's hand and took off down the street. Kelly smiled, picked up the bag, and took off after her. Kelly's long legs seemed to move effortlessly, even holding a couple of grocery bags. She ran with perfect form. She passed Emily just as they got to the front porch.

"You are such a cheater!" Kelly said.

"Hey, I can't help it if you're clumsy."

"Whatever. I still beat you." They laughed as they entered the house.

"That's because I slowed down 'cause I didn't want to mess up your confidence," Emily said. Kelly smiled. Emily baiting her about a race, made her think of her father and their last conversation.

"You may be able to beat me in basketball, but not running," Kelly said, her eyes showing a little sadness.

"That's right, I can beat you in basketball—and don't you forget it!"

"Girl, don't let me start practicing and come out there and take you to the hoop."

"Bring it on," Emily said.

The girls laughed.

"Okay, I do kind of suck in basketball. But if I wanted to I could master it."

"Yeah, right."

"I just don't like running back and forth and stopping. It's like a tease. I like to run as fast as I can and just keep running."

"Hey, you stick to your sport and I'll stick to mine sis'!" Emily said with a smirk. They laughed and shook hands.

As they opened the door, they heard a sniffle and a whimper coming from their mother's room. They looked at each other, they quietly walked down the hall to her room.

They slowly entered, seeing their mother on the phone looking out the window, overcome with emotion.

"I don't know how I feel about this… I miss you, too. You know I love you. I don't know what else to say; I never meant to hurt you," Linda said into the phone, unaware the girls were behind her.

Kelly and Emily were stunned. They continued to watch their mother, horrified by what they were hearing. The girls gasped. Linda turned around, her face full of tears. She quickly turned back around and wiped the tears away. "Uh, let me call you back. I gotta go… oh, oh, okay." She quickly hung up the phone.

The three of them stared at each other.

"Mom, who was that?" Kelly asked, feeling the sting of betrayal. Linda sighed, stepping toward her girls, her nerves getting the best of her.

"Sit down, you guys."

"Mom, what's going on?" Emily asked. "Were you having an affair?" The question rocked Linda. She stood there taken aback. The girls showed their disappointment as they saw the guilt come over their mother's face.

"Just sit down. Both of you."

The girls sat on the bed, heartbroken. Linda sat down beside them. She thought for a moment, wanting to choose her words carefully. "I was talking to my sister." The girls' mouths dropped open at the same time.

"Sister?" Kelly said.

"Yes," Linda replied, apologetic.

"What are you talking about?" Kelly said, baffled.

"Yeah, you don't have a sister," Emily added, bewildered.

"I have a sister. Matter of fact, I have two sisters. And my mom is still alive." The girls were stunned, looking at each other in disbelief.

"But you said, your mom died giving birth," Kelly said, perplexed.

"She didn't," Linda replied.

"Why would you make up something like that?" Emily asked.

"It's complicated."

"Mom, just tell us what's going on." Kelly said, overwhelmed.

"My family never approved of your dad. They thought that I was too young to get married and, frankly, they thought we were making a big mistake. And then I got pregnant. My mom said she never wanted to see me again. Well, actually I said I was running away with your dad and then she said it. Make a long story short. The whole family and I fell out, and I haven't seen any of them in eighteen years."

The girls looked at their mother, feeling like they were in a bad dream. Or maybe just a bad soap opera. "I can't believe this," Emily said.

"Mom, we have a grandmother?" Kelly asked.

"Yes."

"And don't forget, some aunts," Emily said outdone and blown away.

"Well it's better than the alternative," Kelly said.

"That mom was having an affair?"

"Girls, girls. Enough."

"I'm just blown away by all of this," Kelly said.

"This is unbelievable, crazy, ridiculous!" Emily said.

"Ludicrous," Kelly added.

Emily and Kelly looked at each other, stupefied.

"Listen you guys. I am so sorry you had to learn about this, this way. I just wasn't ready to go back and face my mom. It just ended so ugly. I loved your dad so much. I never loved any man like I loved him. And my family and I clashed in a very bad way. And your father and I ran away and never looked back... I just hoped one day I would get the strength to go back and see them. I was just so torn," Linda explained as her daughters stared at her.

Emily looked at her mother as if she was looking at a stranger.

"So what did she say?" Kelly asked.

"Who?" Linda asked.

"Your sister," Emily and Kelly said in unison, nodding to the phone.

Linda thought for a moment.

"She said… come home."

Chapter 4

L inda closed the trunk of her new SUV after the girls said goodbye to a few neighbors, they strolled over to their mother.

Out of nowhere, a fire-red Mustang turned the corner sharply and came to a hard stop in front of their house. Linda and Kelly looked at each other.

"Here we go," Kelly said, wearing a wry smile. Emily looked at the Mustang, shaking her head with embarrassment.

"I hope James doesn't make a scene," Emily said.

"Don't worry, he will," Kelly replied smiling, knowing the treat they were in for.

He was seventeen. He looked like a nerd who was trying to buy popularity points with a cool automobile. He hopped out of his car wearing eyeglasses he probably could read a book across the street with. His blond wavy hair was flipped up with gel holding it in place. And tears ran down his face. He was relieved that they hadn't left yet. He ran to Emily and gave her a hug like he hadn't seen her in ten years.

"Hey," Emily said, hoping he would stop being so dramatic. "I thought you had to work?"

"I did. I just left, though. I had to see you again," James whined. Kelly and Linda looked at each other. They hated when he whined.

"He just saw her last night," Kelly said to Linda. Linda shook her head, amused.

"I know," Linda said matter-of-factly.

James hugged Emily again.

"It's okay, James. We can always talk on the phone," Emily said, a little startled by his intensity.

"I love you, girl. I just wanted to tell you again that I love you, girl." She patted him on the back, feeling awkward in his grasp.

"I love you too, sweetie," she said in a motherly way. "All right already," Emily brushed him off, getting irritated.

Kelly laughed, loving every bit of it.

He wiped his tears and hugged her again passionately. Then he broke down, collapsing on the ground. Emily tried her best to pull him up, then finally stepped back shaking her head, as the pathetic guy sobbed. "What the heck," she said to herself as she watched the show along with everyone else.

Kelly and Linda strolled away. "She should have never taken that boy's virginity," Kelly said, shaking her head, pitying his predicament.

"Will you stop? I don't wanna hear about nobody's virginity being taken," Linda said.

Kelly laughed.

"I'm just saying," she said, amused.

Linda rolled her eyes.

"Well, I still got mine," Kelly said with a smile.

"Good. As you should. You just turned seventeen, for crying out loud." Linda looked back at Emily, trying to help the crying boy off the ground and onto his feet. "Okay, enough of this. I can't take it anymore." Linda called out to Emily, "Sweetie, time to go!"

"Okay," Emily said, trying to comfort the broken-hearted James, rubbing his back as he now sat on the curb about to hyperventilate. He took out his inhaler, shook it, and took a puff.

Linda and the girls put the last of their things in the car, hugged a couple of their neighbors, and pulled away, leaving James sobbing on the curb, his face in his hands.

"You guys sure you didn't forget anything?" Linda asked.

"Nope," Kelly said.

"I got everything," Emily added.

Linda looked at Kelly in the rearview mirror and gave a sly smile.

"You sure, Emily?" Linda said, amused, looking at James in her rearview mirror whaling on the curb. Kelly and Linda busted out laughing as Emily gave a final look at James as they turned the corner. A sadness and a rush of empathy came over Emily. James continued to cry, until a sixteen year old beauty who looked like she could be Emily's sister walked up to him.

"Are you okay?" the young beauty asked. James looked up and smiled brightly.

They traveled for six hours straight. Emily sat in the back seat playing a game on her cell phone while Linda drove with Kelly up front.

"So we're going out here to regroup. I'm going to get a job and save some money, and we're going to start a new life," Linda said, trying her best to sound upbeat.

"Sounds good to me," Emily said without looking up from her phone.

"As long as they got a track team out there, I'm good," Kelly said.

"Trust me, they got track," Linda said.

"As long as they got basketball, I'm good," Emily said.

"They got basketball, too," Linda said. Kelly noticed Emily's sad expression.

"What's wrong?"

"Nothing."

"You thinking about James?"

"A little," Emily said, feeling like a kid who no longer had her puppy to make fetch.

"He'll be all right, you little heartbreaker," Kelly said with a chuckle. "And so will you."

Emily smiled, thinking her sister knew her too well.

"He's probably still crying out in the middle of the street. I know he's going to be calling me all the time."

"Well, you were going to break up with him anyway. He was smothering you."

"Yeah, but I still feel bad. He made me promise to call him as soon as we get there."

"It's okay, sis. He'll call for a while and then eventually get the picture and stop calling."

"I don't know. I'm not that easy to get over."

Kelly gave Emily a dry smile. Linda shook her head, amused by her girls' conversation.

They eventually left the long highway, heading into the hills and through the canyons. The girls stared at farms on the side of the road, where hundreds of cows and sheep grazed.

Emily drove while Linda slept in the back. Kelly looked at her mother sleeping peacefully, like she hadn't slept in weeks. Kelly sighed and turned around. Her mother had been through so much, and if there was anything she could do to make her life easier, she would do it. She loved her mother and wanted to see her happy again. She smiled, thinking that this new start might be just what her mother needed. Actually what they all needed. Kelly thought about her father every day since his passing and knew she wasn't the only one. The accident haunted all of their dreams. And they all struggled to sleep. Victor, for all of them, was like an open wound that would never completely heal.

Chapter 5

T hey drove past a sign that read ten miles to North Carolina. Linda's heart started to race at the thought of seeing her family. Her palms were sweaty and her hands shook. Kelly, noticing mother's nervousness and her shaking hands, gently put her hand on top of her mother's and squeezed it, hoping to ease her tension. Linda smiled.

They pulled up in front of a large two-story colonial-style white house on the corner. It sat on a few acres of land. In the back yard there was at least two hundred yards of fresh-cut grass that only ended at the tree line. Beyond that, was wilderness. Across the street from the house was a bank of homes that led toward the city.

The girls looked on, wide-eyed, as kids in the neighborhood rode their bikes and played football in the street. The folks they assumed were Linda's family seemed to be having a barbeque of sorts. People were eating and kids were playing and almost everyone was wearing dark clothing, which seemed odd for a barbeque. Not quite like a funeral, but not far from it.

Kelly and Emily stared at two women and a man walking by, with the look of hippies. The women's hair was straight as pins, all the way down to their lower backs. The guy had a disheveled curly blond mop. He wore black combat boots, with his jeans tucked inside them. She thought, how different North Carolina is from California.

"Mom, are they having a party?" Kelly asked.

"Nope, just a typical Sunday at my mom's house."

"Man, it's so…. pretty out here," Emily said, looking up at the tall pine trees. "Everything looks so green!"

Linda cut the engine and they just sat there. Linda's nervousness was getting the best of her.

"Mom, you okay?" Emily asked, hugging her from the back seat. Linda didn't answer. She just stared blankly at the people hanging out in the yard.

"Mom, it'll be all right," Kelly said.

Linda snapped out of her trance, pleased to see her girls' excitement.

An attractive woman dressed in mostly black wearing sunglasses, trotted out of the house, staring at the car. She took off her glasses to get a better look. She smiled brightly at the sight of Linda.

"Carrie, she's here!" Brenda yelled back into the house. Linda smiled at the sight of Brenda. The girls got out of the car. Linda was a little slower than the girls to get out, overwhelmed by seeing her younger sister, whom she missed terribly and hadn't seen in eighteen years.

Brenda sashayed over to Linda and jumped into her arms, wrapping her legs around her waist. They hugged, sobbing uncontrollably. The girls watched their mother, full of emotions. Emily tapped Kelly on the shoulder and pointed to a cute boy across the street, who was around their age. He was muscular and handsome. He also had dimples, and the same complexion as Kelly.

"I got dibs," Emily said.

"We'll see about that," Kelly replied. "Besides, aren't you supposed to be in a long-distance relationship?" They laughed. "I think I'm going to like this place," Kelly said as she stared at Thomas who was staring right back, while washing his car.

"You telling me," Emily said, staring at Thomas too.

"He is cute," Kelly said.

"Just 'cause you're both dipped in chocolate doesn't mean he's yours. I saw him first," she said with a smile. Emily watched the two of them stare at each other, smiling. She rolled her eyes. "Fine, take him."

"I will," Kelly said under her breath, still smiling and staring across the street.

Carrie Switch, Linda's older sister, walked out of the house wearing a pleasant smile. "You're home," she said, nowhere near as emotional as Brenda.

Linda took one look at Carrie, wiped her tears away and they hugged. "I missed you, sis'," Carrie said, no longer trying to mask her feelings for her little sister.

"I missed you, too."

Linda's sisters lit up at the sight of Kelly and Emily.

"Well, what do you have here?" Carrie said.

"Carrie, Brenda, meet my girls, Emily and Kelly. Girls, meet my sisters." Linda's sisters hugged the girls.

"Oh my God! She looks just like you, Linda!" Carrie exclaimed, looking at Emily awestruck.

The girls smiled.

"Who? Me or her?" Kelly said with a straight face. Carrie and Brenda looked at each other, then Linda. Emily and Kelly looked at each other, not sure who Carrie was talking about, then they busted out laughing. Carrie and Brenda laughed, getting the joke. Linda shook her head, amused, having heard this bit before.

"I like this girl," Brenda said.

"Funny girl. Well, you got your mom's sense of humor, that's for sure," Carrie said to Kelly. "Welcome to the family, ladies," Carrie said as she hugged the girls again. Carrie did a double-take at Emily's eyes and smiled. She gave Linda a knowing look. Linda looked uncomfortable. "Does she know?" she asked Linda in a hushed tone.

"Know what?" Emily said.

"Nothing, sweetie," Linda said, blowing it off. Kelly and Emily gave each other a strange look. Carrie and Brenda smiled, amused.

"Hmm. Ready to go see mom?" Carrie asked, feeling the tension between the two of them.

"Yeah," Linda said as she exhaled.

"I'll take the girls to meet some of their cousins. Follow me you guys," Brenda said. Linda smiled at her girls as they followed Brenda.

"Come on," Carrie said, taking Linda by the hand and leading her into the house. The two sisters smiled, missing each other, but played it cool not showing too much emotion. However, they both could tell that they were dancing inside with excitement about her being back home.

Brenda took the girls to Uncle Ray first. A man in his late fifties with salt pepper hair, a receding hairline, and a plate full of food. "Uncle Ray, this is Linda's girls."

"Linda's here?" he asked in his deep southern accent.

"Yeah, she just got here," Brenda said, excited. "She's talking to mom." Uncle Ray smiled, happy she finally came back home. He hugged both the girls.

"How you ladies doing? I heard you guys were coming. I hope you're hungry. We got a lot of food, so eat!"

"They will. Bye, Uncle Ray." Brenda laughed. The girls thought he was funny, as he went to a table with his plate of food, jubilant, like a kid rushing to open the big gift at his own birthday party.

They continued through the crowd to the twin girls their age. "Kelly and Emily, these are your cousins, Shonda and Rhonda. Carrie's kids." The girls all shook hands. Shonda and Rhonda were dressed in goth attire, with dark makeup and heavy black eyeliner on. Kelly and Emily were a little taken aback by the twins' outfits and colorful, kooky hairstyles.

"So you guys are from California?" Shonda asked.

"Yep," Emily replied.

"I heard it never rains out there," Rhonda said.

"It rains. Just not that much," Kelly said.

"That's not what we heard," Shonda said.

"Well it does," Emily said.

"But not hard," Rhonda said.

"No, it can rain hard there, too," Kelly said. The twins looked at each other, bewildered.

"Well, we heard it didn't rain at all, maybe just a little sprinkle," Shonda said.

"Yep," Rhonda co-signed.

Kelly and Emily looked at each other and smiled, amused.

"Well, we kind of lived there all our lives," Emily said with a shrug. Kelly nodded in agreement. The twins rolled their eyes a little, as if they still knew better.

Brenda watched, amused by their awkwardness toward each other. She sighed with gratitude, seeing the girls amongst their family. She looked at a family friend chase kids around. He fell over a chair and people laughed hysterically, while helping him up. Their family and friends could be quite festive.

"So, what's there to do around here?" Emily asked, looking around.

"Little this and that," Shonda said.

The four cousins looked at each other, nodding their heads, struggling to make small talk. Brenda stood there, then gave a little chuckle, still pleased to see them getting to know each other in their own way. The twins both noticed Emily's eyes and smirked, amused, giving each other looks. Kelly and Emily looked at each other baffled, not getting the joke.

Carrie and Linda entered the kitchen. Their mother Dorothy stood at the kitchen sink facing a window, with a view of the side yard. She was washing dishes, but stopped at the sound of footsteps behind her. Carrie left so the two of them could talk privately. Dorothy didn't turn around right away, knowing that it was Linda. She was just as nervous as Linda and didn't want to get too emotional. Her hands shook while drying off a plate.

"Hi, momma," Linda said with a tinge of nervousness.

"Hey, sweetie," Dorothy said as she turned around, giving an uncomfortable half smile. Linda's smile mirrored her mother's. She missed being called sweetie by her mother. It was a term of endearment that not only she used but all of the women in her family as well. Even Kelly and Emily used it, not knowing it stemmed from their great-great-grandmother.

"House looks the same." Linda looked around at all of the familiar things in the kitchen.

"Yeah. A few upgrades here and there. But pretty much everything's the same... You have a good drive?"

"Yeah, it was good. My oldest helped out with the drive, so it wasn't so bad."

"She looks like you," Dorothy said, nodding out the back window where she could see Emily and Kelly talking to the twins.

"I get that a lot," Linda said.

"And that's your other daughter?"

"Yeah."

"Well, they're both beautiful."

"Thank you. Mom, I just wanted to say how sorry I am..."

"Sweetie. It's okay. It's been so long, I'm just glad you're home," Dorothy said.

"Me, too." Linda sighed. "Did you think about me while I was gone?"

"Of course I did. But I know how you get."

"What does that mean?" Linda asked.

"You know. When you want something, nothing can get in your way."

"Mom..."

"No, it's okay. That's just your way. You've always been like that, even as a kid."

"But momma, I was in love."

"I know. Sometimes when you become a parent, you lose perspective of what that feels like. And you forget once your children get older they're not yours anymore. They belong to the world."

"I wanted to call home, but the way you cut me off. Well, let's just say, it kind of broke me."

"And when you chose a man over your family, it broke me, too. I don't know. Maybe it's ego. Maybe it's because we love each other so much. I guess we're both just stubborn."

"I do love you," Linda said.

"I know you do. I never doubted that you loved me, or your sisters..."

Linda and Dorothy were at a loss for words for a moment. "I'm sorry about your husband."

"He was the love of my life."

"I know he was."

"I'm so sorry, momma."

"I'm sorry too. You're my baby... You'll always be that. And I'll always love you. Come here." Linda hesitated. "Come."

As Linda slowly walked toward her mother, tears flowed down her cheeks. Dorothy's tears followed.

They held each other in the kitchen for a nice while, taking in the wonderful moment they both longed for. Their hearts were warm and full. And the love in the room was immense.

Chapter 6

M ost of the house lights were off. The neighborhood was darker than a typical neighborhood due to the lack of street lamps. Kelly and Emily put on their pajamas, preparing for bed in the guest bedroom on the second floor. There were four bedrooms upstairs and two bedrooms downstairs and hardwood floors throughout the house.

The girls wrapped their hair in scarves while unpacking their things.

"So, what do you think?" Emily asked.

"They seem nice," Kelly said matter-of-factly.

"Can you believe it? We have a grandmother, aunts, cousins."

"Yeah. I saw mom in the bathroom earlier, crying," Kelly said.

"I know. I talked to her. She said she felt overwhelmed. Imagine if you hadn't seen mom in like eighteen years," Emily said.

Kelly looked around at the dated wallpaper and antique furniture. "I feel like I'm back in time."

"I know. Maybe it's a southern thing," Emily said.

"Yeah. Maybe."

"But what's up with the twins?" Emily said with a humorous smile. "Weird."

"You mean our cousins?" Kelly said, sarcastic. They laughed.

"And what's up with the Goth?"

"I don't know. To each its own," Kelly said with a chuckle. Their eyes moved toward the door, hearing a few taps. "Come in," Kelly said. Linda peeked inside wearing a big smile.

"Hey girls."

"Hey, mom," the girls replied.

"You guys okay?"

"Yeah," Emily said.

"I'm fine," Kelly added.

"So, what do you think? You guys like it here?" she asked, hoping they did.

"I think Kelly likes it here more, especially with that fine... boy across the street," Emily said.

"Shut up," Kelly said.

"Well, tomorrow I'm going to drive you guys around, show you the sites."

"Can we see the school we're going to?" Kelly asked.

"Absolutely."

"Great," Kelly said, wanting to check out the school she would soon become a track star at.

"I know your cousins said they were going to show you around, too."

"What's with them? They seem a little weird," Emily said.

"They're just unique," Linda said.

"Hey, I like unique. Unique is cool," Kelly said.

"Whatever," Emily said.

"All right you guys, get some sleep. Big day tomorrow," Linda said.

"Good night," the girls said. Linda looked at Emily oddly.

"Sweetie, come here."

"What?" Emily said perplexed.

"Come here," Linda reiterated. Emily walked over to her mother. Linda looked into her eyes. Kelly looked at her mother strangely as she examined Emily's pupils and iris.

"What?" Emily said.

"What are you doing?" Kelly asked. Linda continued to search her pretty blue eyes.

"Nothing," Linda said dismissing them. Emily looked at her mother, peculiar. "You look tired. Get some sleep... Good night you guys," Linda said as she headed out of the room.

"Good night," they said once again. Linda closed the door behind her. Kelly and Emily looked at each other.

"What is going on?" Emily said.

"Maybe everyone can tell you're not a virgin," Kelly said with a laugh.

"I should have never told you anything," Emily said.

"Well, too bad. You did," Kelly said with a sardonic expression as she got under the covers.

As the girls fell asleep, darkness consumed the bedroom, shafts of moonlight cutting through the branches of a huge oak tree outside their window. The wind whistled and a twig tapped rhythmically on the windowpane.

The girls were sound asleep, comfortable under their warm sheets and blankets. The room was colder than they were used to and a cold fog escaped their lips with each breath. Then the slow squeaking sounds of the hardwood floors sung from outside their bedroom door. Light spilled into the bedroom as the door creaked its way open. People in black cloaks crept inside. The girls remained asleep as the hooded figures inched their way toward them. But as the wind picked up outside so did the tapping on the window.

Kelly's eyes slowly opened. Still half asleep, she thought that she was seeing things, as shadowy figures filled the room and loomed over her. She blinked hard, trying to get the dark images out of her eyes. She thought that it had to be hair, or lint—something other than what she was seeing. She now heard the squeaking from the hardwood floors and saw the combat boots they all wore. The boots looked familiar to her, in her altered state. Then she heard a *shush* from one of the hooded silhouettes. Her eyes widened. She lay paralyzed, horrified by what she was seeing. Not in a dream. And not in her mind. And nothing in her eyes.

The hooded figures continued to loom over their beds staring down at the girls. One of them put a hand over Emily's mouth and snatched her up. Emily jerked awake out of a dead sleep, kicking and swinging wildly. Kelly hopped up to help Emily but was held on the bed by two large figures. Emily continued to fight, not knowing what was going on, as she was carried out of the room.

Kelly was horrified.

"Don't move," a hooded figure said in a menacing voice.

Kelly lay there, held down, frozen. She stayed still, scared and bewildered, as the hooded figures released her, backed out of the bedroom and closed the door.

Kelly sprung out of bed and landed hard on the floor. She got up rubbing her side, as she stared at the door stunned. The room was again quiet and dark, except for the moonlight, and the forever-tapping twig.

Kelly thought about her next move, still shaken and confused.

"What just happened?" she asked herself. She looked out the bedroom window and saw several shadowy figures, taking Emily toward the woods, with a blanket over her head. She thought to call the police, so she looked at the nightstand where her and Emily's cell phones were last placed. They were no longer there. Kelly scrambled to put on her shoes and rushed down the hall to her mother's bedroom. She flung open the door. "Mom!" No one was there. She quickly realized that all of the bedroom doors were open. She checked each one, but no one was there. She ran down the stairs and found no one down there either. She went into the kitchen, desperately searching for a weapon. She checked some pots and pans hanging from the ceiling, then shook her head. She pulled open drawers looking for a knife. She found a steak knife, but it was too small. Then she grabbed a butter knife, but she wasn't going to be making toast. She scanned the counter and saw an assortment of knives in a wooden block by the microwave. She tossed the other knives aside and rushed to the knife block. She grabbed the biggest one—a butcher knife—and dashed out of the house.

She ran at top speed in her pajamas across the backyard toward the forest, but she had no idea what she would do if she came across the hooded culprits. She asked herself if she could kill someone. She had no idea. All she knew is her sister was in danger and she would do whatever she had to do to save her.

Kelly's eyes got wider, full of fear, as she hit the tree line and entered the pitch-black forest. She bobbed and weaved through the brush, jumping over ditches and rocks. She looked up at the full moon, grateful for the light it supplied as it sliced through the trees. She continued to run until she ran straight into her mother.

"Mom!" Kelly screamed.

"Kelly, what are you doing?" her mother said trying to calm her.

"Mom, some people in hoods took Emily!"

"Kelly..." She looked at the butcher knife Kelly was holding tight in her hand.

"Mom, we don't have time. We have to find her!"

"Kelly! Listen to me."

"What?" Kelly said wild-eyed as she tried to pull her mother along.

"It's okay. Go back to the house," Linda said. Kelly let go of her mother, starring at her in bewilderment.

"But, mom!"

"It's under control. Now go back and get in bed. Trust me. It's okay."

Kelly stared at her mother, still confused.

Linda looked at the knife in Kelly's hand again, then back at her. "It's okay," she said in a calming tone.

Kelly reluctantly turned and headed back to the house.

She lay in bed wide awake, staring at the ceiling. Her door was shut, with the back of a chair jammed under the doorknob. Kelly let her imagination run, thinking maybe her mother was a superhero and that she killed the hooded people. Or maybe this was a prank gone bad and now they were all coming in to break the news. After all, where was the rest of the family? She thought someone would have surely called the police by now if they were in danger.

Maybe it would all turn out to be one big joke. But if it was a joke or prank, it was not funny.

When eventually Emily came back to their room, she was tired and dirty. Kelly sat up and stared at her.

"What the heck happened to you?" Kelly asked, eager to hear the story. Emily walked over and sat down on her own bed in a daze. "Well?" Kelly said, agitated by her silence. Emily looked like she wanted to tell her everything. But instead she shook her head *no*.

"Nothing much."

"What?" Kelly exclaimed.

"Nothing… I mean, I don't remember," Emily said.

"Are you trying to tell me that you don't remember some hooded people coming in here and dragging your butt out in the middle of the night?"

Emily took a moment, not responding, totally out of it.

"Emily, what happened?"

Emily looked at Kelly with lifeless eyes.

"I don't want to talk about it. I can't," Emily stammered.

"What do you mean you can't?"

"I don't wanna talk about it," Emily insisted.

"Well… was mom there?"

Emily sat there stoic.

"This is bull. Anybody try to grab me out of bed is going to have a rude awakening." Kelly whipped out the butcher knife she had hidden under her blanket.

Emily had no reaction. She sighed, still traumatized, and then curled up on the bed in the fetal position facing away from Kelly. Kelly looked at her sister concerned, wondering what the heck was going on. She then did a double-take, noticing their cell phones were back on the nightstand.

Chapter 7

L inda, Emily, and Kelly rode through town. No one said a word. Linda drove acting like everything was okay. Emily sat across from her in a daze. Kelly sat in the back looking at both of them, wondering what was going on. Finally she couldn't take it anymore.

"Is someone going to tell me what's going on?"

Linda and Emily looked at each other, not saying a word.

"Well, fine. Don't say anything. I don't need to know."

"Sweetie. Just relax. Has nothing to do with you," Linda said.

"Fine," Kelly said. She stared straight ahead. Linda suddenly pointed out of her window.

"There's your new high school, you guys."

Kelly and Emily didn't even look.

Kelly sat on the front porch of the Switch house, watching the leaves blowing from the trees. She was in deep thought, trying to understand what was going on and why her mother and sister were keeping her in the dark. She put her face in her hands. When she looked up, she saw Thomas strolling across his lawn to his car. She thought he looked even better looking than when she first saw him. He wore jeans and a tight fitted t-shirt that showed off his muscular arms. She didn't remember him being so buff.

As Thomas grabbed a book bag out of his new Camaro, he saw Kelly staring at him. He gave her a wave and a smile. Kelly waved back, her mouth slightly open. When she realized her mouth was open, she quickly shut it. Thomas strolled back to his house, continuing to make eye contact with Kelly. When he got to his front door he suddenly stopped, reeled around and headed across the street toward Kelly. She got up and met him at the curb. "Hey, how's it going?" Thomas asked.

"Fine," Kelly replied with a smile.

"My name's Thomas."

"Hmm. You don't look like a Thomas."

"What does that mean?"

"I don't know, you just don't," Kelly said, swallowing the lump in her throat. They both gave a nervous chuckle.

"So what's your name?"

"Kelly."

"You don't look like a Kelly, you look more like a Tina."

She smiled, amused. "Whatever," she said, dismissing his poor attempt at a comeback. They laughed.

"So you guys moved in or just visiting?" Thomas asked, trying to be as charming as possible.

"I guess you can say moved in. At least for a little while."

"Where are you from?"

"California. San Diego to be exact."

"So you're a California girl. I could kind of tell you were from the west coast."

"Really. How?"

"Because of the way you and your sister have your hair. All... done, I guess."

"What? The girls out here don't do their hair?" Kelly said, with a smirk.

"Not like that, all professional and stuff."

"I think you're just used to looking at the twins, Rhonda and Shonda."

He laughed.

"You might be right. Maybe I've been swayed by their spiked Goth hairstyles." He smiled as if he had his own lightbulb moment. "I know what it is. You guys have long hair. A lot of the girls out here keep their hair cut short. Well, at least shorter than yours."

"Is long hair a bad thing?"

"No, that's a good thing."

They stood there smiling and flirting, rocking back and forth on the heels of their shoes. "So, how do you like it here so far?"

"It's okay. Kind of slow, but cool."

"Yeah. Are the Switchs' your family?"

"Yeah."

"Adopted?" he asked. Kelly gave him her traditional "duh" expression. "Okay, that was stupid," he acknowledged, amused.

"It's cool. I've just kind of heard it about a thousand times growing up."

"Yeah, you kind of lose some smart points when you ask that, I guess," Thomas said with a smile.

"Just a little."

They laughed.

Thomas thought that Kelly was even more beautiful now that he was closer. He liked her smile, especially her lips.

"Well, feel free to come by if you ever get bored. Or you need someone to show you around," he said.

"Okay."

"You know where I live," Thomas said, slowly backing away.

"And you know where I live."

"I do. So, see you around," he said, surprised that he was a little nervous.

"Bye," Kelly said with a wave.

Thomas smiled and started to walk away, but then stopped and turned around.

"What are you doing tonight? I have a friend who's having a house party," he said, almost as if it was a challenge.

"A house party?"

"Yeah, if you want, you can come. You and your sister."

"Well, I don't know about my sister, but I'm down."

"You're down?" Thomas said. She nodded. "See, you even talk different." His dimples got even deeper when he smiled. "So, I'll pick you up tonight."

"Why don't I just pick you up? It would be easier to just walk across the street, since you're driving."

"Okay, let me see your phone."

She handed him her phone. He took it and quickly typed his cell number into it. "There you go. So be at my house at about ten."

"Ten?"

"Too late for you?"

"No, ten's fine," Kelly said.

Thomas smiled and strolled away.

"See you tonight," he said.

Kelly waved and walked back to her porch. They turned around at the same time and smiled.

Kelly went through her clothes and pulled out a couple different outfits. She held a blouse up to her chest and looked in the mirror, making sure that the color scheme worked. She wanted her outfit to be sexy but not too revealing. She smiled at her reflection, then a sadness came over her. She thought about her dad. Then her mother and sister. She felt like a person without a country trying to find someone who would tell her that things were going to be okay and that she was not alone.

Emily walked in. She looked at Kelly, nicely dressed and putting makeup on.

"Where you going?" she asked.

"Are you serious?" Kelly replied, thinking her sister had some nerve to ask her anything.

"What?" Emily shrugged.

Kelly stopped and turned around.

"You're asking me a question?" Kelly snapped.

"Fine," Emily said, looking away.

"You and mom. I don't know what the heck is going on with you guys."

"Talk to mom."

"I'm not talking to mom. I'm talking to you. What's going on?"

Emily didn't answer.

"Whatever. I'm done," Kelly said, staring back in the mirror continuing with her makeup. Emily lay down on her bed, staring at the ceiling. Kelly saw her in the mirror. Their eyes met. Kelly cut her eyes at her, then left.

Kelly strolled across the street, texting Thomas on her phone, *I'm out front.* She looked beautiful, wearing tight fitted jeans and boots with a blouse that showed off her cleavage. She knew she had an amazing body, thanks to her obsession with track. And she wanted Thomas to know he wasn't the only one with a great physique. Besides, she knew that her sister was a boy magnet and had her eye on Thomas too.

Thomas strolled out wearing a huge smile as he read her text on his phone.

"I know. I saw you from my window," Thomas said, amused. They beamed at the sight of each other. He looked her up and down, showing his dimples. "You look nice." He liked her cute smile and her long hair, now down her back and curled.

"Thank you. You don't look so bad yourself."

Thomas wore fitted jeans and a button-down shirt. Kelly also noticed that he had a fresh haircut. She wondered if he got it cut because of her. His hair had waves and was faded on the sides. She thought he was gorgeous.

"So, you ready to go have a good time?" he asked.

"Sure, lead the way."

Thomas opened the passenger door. After Kelly got in he closed the door, walked around and jumped in. As he drove, Kelly checked out the interior lights that danced across the dashboard.

"Nice car," Kelly said, feeling like she was in a spaceship as he accelerated through a yellow light.

"Thanks. But the car note is killing me."

"Hey, you only live once."

"Yeah, I ain't gonna front. I love it."

Thomas whipped around the corner where a throng of teenagers filled the streets. Some of them were drinking, acting crazy, dancing on the sidewalks.

Thomas pulled over and parked. As the two of them strolled down the street toward the party, they came across two of Thomas's buddies, Jacob and Leonard.

"Thomas, what's up?" Jacob said.

"Nothing much," Thomas replied.

"Who's your friend?" Leonard asked, looking at Kelly.

"This is Kelly. Kelly, this is Leonard and Jacob."

"What's up?" the guys said.

"Hey," Kelly replied with a wave.

"So how's the party?" Thomas asked.

"It's off the hook. D Jay Mammoth is here," Jacob said.

"And the honeys are everywhere," Leonard said, brimming with excitement.

Kelly was amused. She thought Leonard was corny. But to her most guys were.

"So, are we going in or what?" Jacob asked.

"No doubt," Thomas said.

"You guys have a lot of house parties out here?" Kelly asked.

"That's all we have," Leonard said.

"In Cali, the police would have broke this party up," Kelly said.

"They get broke up out here, too, so let's get in there before it does," Thomas said. They continued down the street picking up their pace.

The packed house was full of teenagers dancing to loud music. Kelly and Thomas looked more like observers as they posted up against a wall.

Random people came up to Thomas, shaking his hand. He loved the attention he was getting—from the girls who liked him and the guys who wanted to be like him. He was a high school football star who was charming, handsome, and very nice to everyone. The only fight he ever had was defending a boy being bullied by another kid.

"Somebody's popular," Kelly said.

"It's a football thing," Thomas said, feeling himself.

"So you play football?"

"Yep."

"What position?"

"Strong safety."

"Cool."

"You play sports?"

"Yep."

"Let me guess. Basketball."

"Nope. Track."

"Track?" He looked her up and down. "I could see that," he said impressed.

"Oh you can," Kelly said, flirting a little as his eyes scanned her backside.

"So, can you dance or just run fast?" Thomas asked while bobbing his head to the beat of the music.

Kelly gave him a look that said *don't insult me*.

They danced having a good time. Although both were good dancers, they laughed at each other battling dance moves. Their eyes smiled, impressed with each other's moves.

"Having fun?" Thomas asked, Kelly, knowing she was.

"Uh... yeah," she said, forgetting all of her problems for the moment.

They continued to dance, eyes fixed on each other. Suddenly Kelly looked away, focusing behind Thomas on three people entering the party. It was the twins Shonda and Rhonda, accompanied by Emily. All three of them dressed Goth. "What the?" Kelly said, focused especially on Emily's new attire.

Thomas turned around.

"Ain't that your sister?"

Kelly stared at Emily, not believing what she was seeing.

"I guess."

Emily looked uncomfortable in her new outfit and dark makeup.

The three Goth girls strolled through the party. All eyes were on them.

"Thomas, I gotta get some air," Kelly said, as she continued to stare at Emily.

They headed out to the backyard. Teenagers hung out talking, some smoking cigarettes.

Kelly, flustered, strolled over to a table with a punch bowl. She poured herself a cup.

"Be careful with that."

"Why?"

"It might have something a little more than punch in it."

"Well, if it does, I need it." She gulped the drink down. Thomas smiled. She smiled back. "Just what the doctor ordered. Want some?"

"Nah, I'm driving," he said, amused.

"Okay," she said.

He thought she was cute as she poured and downed another cup.

"You are funny. And you can drink."

"I know, and I'm not even a drinker."

"Could have fooled me."

"Seriously, this is the second drink I've ever had in my life. Dude, I'm an athlete. And a good girl."

"Well you look like an athlete, but I don't know about a good girl," he said with a smile. She put the drink down.

"I am a good girl, Thomas," she said, with sincerity. Her eyes went to the twins and her sister as they stepped out of the house and into the backyard.

"Are you okay?" Thomas asked.

"Yeah, I'm fine."

His eyes followed hers to the three girls in black.

"What's the matter? Family kind of freaking you out?"

"You have no idea."

"Look, don't sweat it. You're going to hear it all. Especially when you get to school. They're going to say your family's a bunch of witches. Some people are going to say devil worshippers. Just ignore it."

"What are you talking about?"

"People say your family are witches and devil worshippers."

"Are you serious?"

"Yeah," he said matter-of-factly.

"Have you ever seen them do anything strange like that?"

"No. Except for the fly Goth gear," Thomas said, chuckling. Kelly was not amused. "But me and my dad just moved into our house three years ago."

"Where's your mom?"

"She left my dad two months after we moved in. She went off to Hollywood to be an actress. My dad said she had a midlife crisis. She calls a couple times a year."

"Sorry to hear that."

"Hey, it is what it is." Thomas shrugged it off, but Kelly could see the pain in his eyes. "Remember, you came to have a good time, not hear my sob stories."

"That's true," Kelly said, as if he was right, lightening the mood. They laughed.

"You're funny," Thomas said.

"Yeah, people tell me that, so back on me."

"You really are funny."

They laughed again.

"My sister and my mom are just freaking me out. And as far as my new cousins I don't know them from a can of paint. Hey, you're the neighbor. You tell me what's up with them?"

"The twins, yeah, they're kind of weird. But, hey, I like weird. It's more interesting than being like everyone else."

Kelly looked at him, knowing she said something similar.

"Yeah, me too," Kelly said with a smile. "I just hope I can make it here. I'm just going to look at it this way: in another year I'll graduate and be in college on a track scholarship."

"You're that fast?"

"Ah, yeah," she said with a cocky smile.

"I guess you look fast for a girl," he said, taunting her. Kelly smiled.

"I already got nine offers for scholarships."

"Damn, you must be really good then," he said, "Yeah, I only got seven... I mean twenty-seven scholarship offers."

She smiled.

"Well, you're looking at a future gold medalist. But I don't like to brag."

They laughed.

"Hey, that's cool." Thomas was impressed. "You're all right. You just have to loosen up, that's all."

"What makes you think I need to loosen up?"

"You just do."

She smirked.

"I can help you with that," Thomas said, flirting.

"I'm good," she replied with suspicious eyes.

"Not like that," he said, seeing that his words were taken out of context.

"I don't know about you." She gave a quizzical expression, but her eyes flirted back.

"I'm just saying. I'll look after you and make sure you have some fun," Thomas said with a smile. "You'll be my little project." He grabbed her by the waist and pulled her in to him. They laughed as she pushed him back.

"Hmm. We'll see about that," Kelly said, blushing.

"Hey, cousin," Rhonda said to Kelly. Kelly was thrown off by the girls in black, who approached out of nowhere.

"So, you met Thomas?" Shonda said.

"Yes I did," Kelly replied matter-of-factly.

"Thanks for taking our cousin out, Thomas," Rhonda said.

"That's what neighbors are for," he said with a smile. "And how are you ladies doing this beautiful night?" He tried his best to be as enchanting as possible, feeling the tension in the air.

"Good," the twins said together.

Kelly and Emily looked at each other. Emily was being unusually quiet.

"Nice outfit, Emily," Kelly said with a hard look.

"Shonda and Rhonda thought it would be cool," Emily said, embarrassed by her new wardrobe choice.

"Well it is. It's a good look for you," Kelly said wearing a satirical smile.

"Thanks," Emily said, aware of the sarcasm in her tone.

Shonda and Rhonda looked at each other, amused. They all stood silent letting the tension grow.

"Well, you ready, Kelly?" Thomas said finally, keeping his promise and looking after her. Kelly smiled.

"Yeah."

Thomas extended his hand and she grabbed it. When their hands clasped, they felt a strange sensation that was electric. Their eyes acknowledged it and they smiled. Emily and the twins noticed their chemistry too.

As they walked out, Kelly looked back at Emily, who seemed lost. Kelly thought that something was definitely wrong. Emily stood there like someone waiting to be thrown a lifeline.

Thomas and Kelly left the party behind them and rode up into the hills. They parked, overlooking the city. There were a few other cars parked there as well. Thomas turned off the engine and they let out a big sigh. As she took in the view of the twinkling city lights, Kelly smiled.

"Did you just bring me to a makeout spot?" Kelly said amused.

"Yeah, but that's not why I bought you up here. Just wanted to show you the view." She looked at him unsure of his intentions.

"It's beautiful," she said, nodding. He smiled, glad she appreciated it. She still wondered if it was the view he loved or the make-out session he thought he was going to have.

"Yeah it is beautiful. Especially at night," Thomas said, sighing. "I love it up here. My mom brought me here when we first got to town. She said this is where dreams are created." He gave a smirk at the thought of his mother.

"I can see dreams being made here," Kelly said.

"What's yours?" Thomas asked.

"I want to win a gold medal. And become a mom. Wife. You know, have a family."

"Well close your eyes and make a wish."

"Huh?"

"You heard me," Thomas said.

Kelly smiled, a little embarrassed, then finally closed her eyes. She kept them closed for a nice moment. Then a tear rolled down her cheek. She opened her eyes. She wished her father was still alive.

"You okay?" Thomas asked.

"Yeah," she said wiping the tear away.

"You sure?"

"Yes."

"You want to talk about it?" She thought about it.

"No. Some other time maybe."

Thomas put his arm around her and gently kissed her on the forehead, comforting her.

"You're not putting the moves on me, are you?" Kelly asked.

"Kelly, if I was putting the moves on you... you'd know."

She leaned into him as they sat in the car admiring the view that inspires dreams.

Emily rode in the back seat of the twins' mother's SUV. She stared out the window thinking about her new wardrobe and the look on her sister's face when she saw it. She was never the follower type, but she let the twins talk her into it. She was lost and she knew it. Like a leaf blowing in the wind with no direction. Emily wore a sour expression, knowing that if she knew Kelly was going to be at the party, she would have never worn that outfit, or the make-up, no matter how much the twins deemed it necessary. She felt humiliated.

"You okay back there?" Shonda said.

"I'm fine."

"You sure, Emily?" Rhonda said.

"Yeah, I'm fine." Emily wasn't fine. She felt like screaming and crying at the same. She didn't even know where they were going.

"It's a pretty night, you guys," Shonda said, rolling down her window and letting the warm wind go through her fingers.

"Where are we going?" Emily asked.

"Don't worry about it..." the twins said in unison.

"You know, I think I want to go home."

"We are not taking you home," Shonda said matter-of-factly.

"Why not?"

"We're already out. You'll get home soon enough," Rhonda said.

"Well, drop me off at a bus stop and I'll get back that way."

The twins looked at each other and rolled their eyes. Shonda, who was driving, gave a smile to Rhonda and shrugged. They were amused.

"Okay," Shonda said.

Emily was perplexed… wondering what Shonda was saying *okay* to.

"Here's a bus stop up ahead." Rhonda pointed.

Emily was in disbelief that they were actually dropping her off at almost midnight.

Shonda pulled over and came to an abrupt stop right in front of the bus stop.

"All right. This bus should take you home I think," Shonda said.

Emily hesitated, stunned for a moment, then got out of the car. As soon as she got out, Shonda punched it and drove off.

Emily stood alone on the street corner, watching the twins drive away. She looked around, realizing this was not the safest place to be. She pulled out her phone, thinking if she wanted to call her mom to come get her. She then thought about calling her sister, but she definitely didn't want to humiliate herself any further. She looked around, realizing there weren't any buses in sight. She sat on the bench, thinking about what her next move should be. She started to dial her mother…

Tires screeched. Emily jumped, almost dropping her phone.

"Will you get your silly butt in the car? You know darn well ain't no buses running this late," Rhonda said. She opened the door for her to get in. Emily thought for a moment, wondering if she was better off on the street corner. The twins laughed.

She rolled her eyes and got in and they drove off.

"Look, if you have to know, we're going to another party," Shonda said.

"A better party," Rhonda added. The girls smiled at each other amused. Emily was irate, not getting the joke and wanting to just go home but she said nothing.

They finally pulled up to an extravagant home in the hills, overlooking the city. It was a mid-century home, beautifully landscaped. Even though there were only a few cars out front, they could hear music blaring.

Rhonda turned to Emily.

"Look, if anyone asks you if you're a part of the craft, just say yes," Rhonda said.

"But don't talk about the craft like you know it, okay?" Shonda added.

"How about I just wait in the car?"

"No, because that would be just weird," Rhonda said with a smirk. "Now get out," Rhonda said eager to go inside.

They headed up the walk to the front door. Shonda knocked.

They were greeted by a man wearing a black robe with tattoos on his face, and a couple of face piercings. A woman walked by and smiled at them. She was wearing a long black dress, in a spectacular display of Goth. The house was dark, with red lights spinning and flashing throughout. There were only about sixteen people there. Some were dancing. Some just stood around talking.

Emily followed them inside. She made small talk with some of the people she met, while watching the twins socialize in their element. A couple kissed by the kitchen. They looked like vampires. She wondered if the blood pumping through her veins was safe here. Maybe they were all waiting for a signal and would turn on her all at the same time and have her for dinner, sucking her blood until her heart stopped. She shivered at the thought. Or maybe she was just being overly dramatic, and this was more like a Halloween party, just not on Halloween. But she did know better. This was the twins' everyday attire. And these were their people, whether they were family or not.

She leaned against the wall, watching people mingle. She stayed there most of the night because she didn't trust any of them, including her cousins. She had no idea where the night would lead. All she knew is that it was going to be a long one. She looked at a clock on the wall. It read 1:19 a.m.

Kelly's clock on the wall read 4:43 a.m. She was asleep, but stirred when she heard a sound. Her eyes fluttered, registering the squeaks from the old wood floors. Suddenly, she popped up in bed, eyes wide open. The door was closed. She looked over at the bed next to her. Emily was sound asleep. Kelly sighed and lay back down.

Suddenly, the door busted open. Kelly sat up again with a start, terrified. People with hoods on rushed in and grabbed her out of bed. Kelly tried to fight, but she was overpowered. She looked at Emily who just lay sleep, but then opened her eyes, staring at her with no expression. Kelly kicked and screamed. Emily did nothing to stop them. Kelly continued to fight as she was being dragged out of the room.

"Emily, help me! Help!"

Emily rose and pulled the cover off, revealing the same hooded outfit. Kelly's eyes went even wider at the sight of Emily's cloak. "Emily, what are you doing?" Kelly screamed as they dragged her out of the room.

They carried Kelly through the woods screaming and kicking, until one of the hooded figures lost his grip, allowing Kelly to break away. Kelly ran at top speed, horrified.

"Let's kill her!" one of the hooded figures shouted. They all chased her. Kelly ran like the track star she was. They were right on her heels. Kelly hurtled over broken branches at top speed. She was surprised at how fast they were, and how they were all catching up to her.

Suddenly, she ran right into Linda, who stabbed her in the belly with a butcher knife. Their eyes locked, staring into each other's souls.

"Momma..." Kelly said, in hitched breath. Linda's eyes were apologetic. Kelly looked down at the blade in her stomach, bewildered. The blade was an inch above her navel, and blood flowed out of her wound with no sign of stopping. Kelly's eyes went wide as she tried to stop the blood with her hands, making them bloody as well...

"Momma!" Kelly screamed as she woke up in bed with a gasp, holding her stomach. She could feel her heart beating out of her chest as she took in gulps of air, trying to catch her breath. Kelly checked her hands for blood, then her stomach for a wound. There was neither blood or a wound.

She looked over at Emily, who was in her bed asleep.

Chapter 8

T he next morning Thomas's doorbell rang. When he answered, Kelly was there, looking shook up.

"Can you talk?" Kelly asked, her nerves still on edge from the nightmare she had last night.

"Yeah. What's up?" He opened the door wider for her to enter. She stepped inside.

"You here alone?"

"Yeah, why?" he said a little concerned.

"I don't know. I just need to talk to someone," she said.

"Kelly, what's wrong?"

She hesitated before responding.

"Do you have a computer?" she asked.

"Yeah."

They went into his den and turned on his computer.

"I don't know what's going on over there, but I think my family might be in a cult, or witches, or devil worshippers or something," Kelly said as she ran her fingers across Thomas's keyboard.

"Kelly, they're not witches. They're probably just in a book club."

"Really. A book club?"

"Sure."

"Books, my butt." She googled *witches* and *devil worshippers*.

Information on devil worshippers and witches started to display on Thomas's computer. Thomas looked on, skeptical, thinking Kelly was overreacting.

Kelly read about spells. She also read about the history of devil worshippers and witches in America. She found particularly interesting that in the late 1800s thousands of innocent people were burned at the stake because they were thought to be witches. When in actuality they were free thinkers and healers, and in some cases people who just wanted to help other people in need. She read about present-day witches. A lot of them wore Goth attire with dark makeup. This peeked her interest.

"Kelly, what do you expect to find?"

"I don't know," she said, not sure of anything.

She then clicked over to YouTube and watched a group of witches on the beach chanting, putting a spell on a person standing in the middle of a circle. Her eyes focused as she saw that person start to have a seizure and convulse, as the witches continued to chant to climax, screaming with their hands high in the air. Then the people on the beach erupted in laughter. She read the comments on the video spoof. Some commented favorably on the practical jokers and others said they were going to a special place in hell for their joke. She clicked and continued on with her search. Hours went by.

Thomas stared out the window looking at kids at play in the streets. After a minute he returned to Kelly and looked on as she continued to read and watch videos, uneasy. Spells, rituals, costumes, and even weapons.

"Are you okay?" he asked.

"I think this stuff is starting to freak me out."

"Don't sweat it. Most of the stuff on the Internet is fake anyway. Just talk to your mom. Ask her what's going on with them."

"I tried. She's not telling me anything."

"What do you think is wrong?" Thomas asked.

Kelly thought for a moment.

"I don't know. Maybe they're all in a religious cult."

"Look, as long as I've been here, I've never seen any witches burned, black magic or devil worshipping. And definitely no praying to the stars at night. Just bad dressing," Thomas said matter-of-factly.

Kelly chuckled and let out a big sigh.

"Look, a few nights ago, some hooded people came into me and my sister's room in the middle of the night and took Emily out into the woods."

Thomas cracked a smile as if she was joking. However, she didn't smile back. His smile quickly disappeared.

"Are you serious?" Thomas said.

"Yeah. They took her out in the woods."

"For what?"

"I don't know, no one will tell me. Not even my sister."

"What do you mean no one will tell you?"

"They all act like it never happened."

"Well maybe it was a bad dream."

"No. Dreams is what I've been having ever since. More like nightmares."

"Wow."

"Scariest moment in my life. I ran out in the woods with a butcher knife to go help my sister. And my mom stopped me. And she just told me to go back home. She said she had everything under control and to trust her. But I don't trust her anymore. 'Cause something's not right. I don't know what it is, but something in that house just isn't right."

Thomas listened attentively.

"The next time something goes down, call me."

"What are you going to do?" she asked as if he couldn't do anything.

Thomas pulled her away from his computer. "Come with me." He led her up the stairs.

"Uh, where are we going?"

"To my room."

"I'm not going to your room."

"Kelly, trust me."

He continued to guide her.

"You better not be trying to put the moves on me."

"I'm not. And like I said before, if I was… you'd know. Now are you going to let me show you something or not?"

"All right." They went to his bedroom. He grabbed a flashlight out of his closet, then pointed out of his window. Across the street they could see the inside of the hallway at the Switch house.

"If you go to that hallway window I can see you. So just flash this light in that window and I'll come running."

"What are you, a peeping Tom-Thomas?" He laughed.

"No. Never had a reason to look. Until now."

She smiled.

"I got your back. Just sleep light and call me if something happens." Kelly looked into his eyes and felt a little bit safer. She kissed him on the lips softly. "Did you just put the moves on me?" Thomas asked with a smile.

"What do you think?" she replied with an even bigger smile. She kissed him again longer and harder. When they finally stopped kissing, they backed up to let things cool off a bit.

"That was nice," Kelly said.

"That *was* nice," Thomas replied, licking his lips, tasting the peach lip gloss from Kelly's lips. He shook his head, a little dizzy and nervous from the kiss. "So, like I said, just flash this light from there." Thomas pointed back to the Switch house.

To their surprise, Dorothy stood at her window peering back at them, like a frozen statue with big rollers in her hair. Thomas quickly pushed Kelly out of her line of sight and ducked himself. They stood behind the wall, away from the window, alarmed. Then laughed hysterically as they hid from the peering eyes of Dorothy Switch.

"Your grandmother creeps me out," Thomas said as he drove Kelly down a back street where there was a bunch of small businesses—antique stores, bookstores, clothing stores, and second-hand shops. Kelly studied the addresses of the stores as the numbers decreased.

"Yeah, she was looking a little weird with them rollers in her head." They laughed as they continued down the street.

"Yes she was."

"I just want my life back. I just want to be normal and finish school."

"Well, you're pretty far from being normal, Kelly."

"You have jokes?"

"I mean that in a good way."

"Oh, because it sounded like an insult," Kelly said with a smirk.

"I think you just like to fight," Thomas said.

"Well, maybe I do. What can I say? I'm a fighter."

"Maybe you just haven't hung out with a real man to put you in your place."

"Oh, really. I'd love to see you try." She gave him a playful punch in the arm.

"Hey, I'm driving here!"

They laughed.

"Sorry."

"I take driving very serious," he said with a straight face. She mirrored his serious face until he smiled.

They pulled in front of what appeared to be a bookstore. It looked like it was out of business.

"Are you sure about this?" Thomas said as he parked.

"People on line say this is the place to go to. Let's just check it out." Thomas looked like he wasn't sure about any of this. "What, you scared?"

"Girl, please."

Thomas got out of the car. Kelly smiled and got out as well.

The creepy little bookstore was called *Coven's Delight*. As they entered, they set off a string of bells that hung from the door. That got the attention of the owner, who stood behind the cash register wearing a warm smile, dressed in black from head to toe.

Kelly perused the store with Thomas in tow. She looked through books titled *Spells That Kill*, *The Devil's Playground*, *Living With Witchcraft*, and *Modern Day Vampire*.

"Vampire? Really?" Thomas said.

"Hey, you never know."

Thomas looked at photographs with different witchcraft signs with their meanings on the back.

"Kelly, come check this out." He showed her some pictures. There was the Pentacle symbol—a star with a circle around it. There was also the fire symbol, which was a triangle, and the water symbol, which was a triangle upside down, and many other random symbols.

Kelly looked on wide-eyed, wanting answers so bad. She hoped she would see something that was familiar. She thought about the pictures on the walls in the Switch house—nothing resembled any of these signs of witchcraft or devil worship. She sighed hard, looking at the Pentacle symbol again, examining it from different angles.

The owner saw Kelly looking through the photographs, more eager than normal, searching for answers. She gracefully came over to Kelly, and looked at the symbols she appeared to be interested in.

"You want some help, sweetie?"

Kelly was thrown off for a moment at being called *sweetie* by such a grim lady. Also the word *sweetie* was her family's word.

"No thank you. Well, actually, do a lot of people buy this stuff?"

The owner responded with a cold smile.

"I'm sorry, not like that. It's just, it all seems so weird, I mean unique."

"Well, it's definitely not for everyone. Do you study the craft?"

"No. Oh God, no."

The woman smiled again.

Kelly looked at the star and half moon on her necklace, realizing she just insulted the woman once again. "I mean no."

"It's okay."

"Do you have devil worshipping symbols?"

The woman smiled.

"Of course, my child. If I have God symbols, why wouldn't I have his adversary's?" she said as if she was discussing recipes in a cookbook.

She went over the symbols more in-depth, freaking Kelly and Thomas out at times and making them want to laugh at others. She was irritated by their amusement at some of the things she was telling them. She gave Kelly a cold stare, making sure she understood the seriousness and weight of what she was telling her.

"You know, you have to admire the devil. He's so hated by so many, and yet still so incredibly powerful."

"Only powerful to someone who gives him that power," Kelly said.

"And you can admire a snake. That doesn't mean you want to be one," Thomas said.

The woman looked at them first with irritation, then with the warm smile she gave them when they entered the store.

"You folks are young and haven't lived long enough."

"You don't have to live long to know good from evil."

She stared at them, not saying a word. She sensed something in them.

"Well, nice to meet you." She reached her hand out. Kelly hesitated, but then extended her hand. The woman held Kelly's hand for a few seconds too long before Kelly pulled it back. The woman's eyes closed, as if she was downloading Kelly's future. The woman opened her eyes and smiled.

"I have a strong feeling that you will someday learn the essence of true evil. And you will feel the devil's wrath like most people will never know in their lifetime."

Kelly and Thomas looked at the woman as if she was crazy. The woman chuckled and strolled away.

"Thomas, what's wrong with North Carolina?"

"Hey, this is all news to me."

As the owner walked away, she shivered hard twice as if trying to shake off a bad spirit. Kelly and Thomas looked at each other.

"I think I've seen enough. Maybe you're right. Maybe they're just part of some weird book club," Kelly said to Thomas as they walked out of the store. But in her heart she knew that the Switch family was more likely to be aliens than members of a book club.

Something was not right. She just didn't know what.

Chapter 9

K elly and Emily slept peacefully. The clock on their nightstand read 3:02 a.m. Emily suddenly opened her eyes and pulled back her covers. She was fully dressed in all black and wearing combat boots. She eased out of bed and crept out of the room. As soon as the door closed, Kelly's eyes opened. She hopped out of bed and quickly put on some jeans and a sweatshirt. She grabbed her cell phone and called Thomas. The phone rang four times before he answered it, half asleep.

"Hello?" Thomas said, eyes still closed.

"Emily just left. Meet me out back."

"Huh?" he said, trying to get his bearings.

"Just meet me in my backyard where the forest begins."

"Are you serious?" He sat up, looking at the clock on his wall.

"Yes!"

"All right, all right!"

Kelly headed out of the room.

She ran toward the tree line, trying to tell if she could see anyone in the woods. She saw no one, but she heard what sounded like a faint humming deep in the woods. She waited for Thomas. About five minutes had passed. She wondered if he went back to sleep. She was scared to go into the woods by herself but she desperately had to know what was going on. Just as she was about to go alone, she saw Thomas jogging toward her with his flashlight on. She smiled, relieved.

"Thanks for coming," Kelly said, nervous and cold. "Turn that light off, though. They'll see us coming."

"Who?"

"My family."

"You sure about this?"

"Absolutely."

He looked around.

"Are you sure they're out here?"

"Yeah."

"It's freezing." He looked into the woods, daunted by the darkness.

"If you're scared, you can go back," she said with a nervous smile.

"Scared? Please." She smirked, knowing he was a little. But so was she. "I just don't wanna get mauled by a bear, that's all. Or Bigfoot." They let out nervous chuckles.

"We have to hurry... ready to run?" Kelly asked.

"Sooner we see what's up, the sooner I can get back in bed. Let's do it," Thomas said.

"Try to keep up."

"Please!" Thomas exclaimed.

Kelly took off with Thomas right behind her. They dashed through the woods.

"Jeez," Thomas said to himself as she started to pull away. He kicked it into a higher gear to catch up. Kelly was impressed by his speed as well.

She looked up at the light supplied by the moon. They ran as fast as they could until they saw some flickering lights. They slowed down and inched as close as they could without being detected.

They could see lit candles held by people wearing cloaks. The hoods covered most of their faces, so Kelly and Thomas couldn't recognize any of them.

"What the heck is this?" Thomas said, eyes wide in disbelief.

"I told you."

"This your family?"

"Yeah."

"What are they doing?"

"I have no idea. I'm hiding behind a freaking bush just like you," Kelly said, her mouth gaped open, heart beating out of her chest.

"This is crazy. Maybe we should go back," Thomas said.

"No, I need to find out what's going on," Kelly said, not believing what she was seeing.

The cloaked people formed a circle and then began taking down their hoods, revealing themselves. The whole Switch family was there.

Emily was the last one to reveal herself. She stood alone in the middle of the circle. Linda stood next to her mother.

Kelly looked on in awe. "What are they doing?" she said to herself.

Together the Switch family chanted, "May the gods be kind and show their light," while looking up to the sky.

"Lay the child on the ground," Dorothy said. Brenda and Carrie lay Emily down.

"Free yourself, sweetie," Linda said.

Kelly watched, horrified, feeling like an outsider to the only family she had. She could not believe her mother had kept her family a secret. And now this. Tears filled her eyes as she struggled to comprehend it all.

Kelly became more and more emotional.

"Let's go, Kelly," he said in a hushed voice. "This is getting too weird."

"No, I have to see everything."

Dorothy placed her hand on Emily's shoulder, then the rest of the family placed their hands on Emily's shoulder as well.

"Emily Switch, do you accept your family from now until eternity?" Dorothy asked. The fact that she used the name Switch instead of their birth name Paterson shook Kelly to her core. She tried to swallow the lump in her throat.

"Yes," Emily said, as if she was surrendering to the power of her whole family's energy.

"Do you accept your powers as a gift from your creator and great ancestors and beyond?"

"Yes!" she exclaimed.

"Do you accept being a member of the Switch family, and all that comes with it?"

"Yes," Emily cried out, as the energy wracked her body sending her head back and forth.

Kelly watched, mesmerized, forgetting to breathe. She stared at Emily's head as it swayed back and forth until she looked like she was going to pass out.

"Congratulations, Emily. You are one of us," Dorothy said in a calm, pleasant voice.

Emily's body crumpled but everyone was waiting to catch her. Her body was limp and her eyes welled up as the Switch family chanted, "You are one of us."

Kelly was numb. She didn't know whether she should be horrified or jealous, as the Switch family continued to chant, "You are one of us." Suddenly Emily rose from their hands and into the air.

"You gotta be kidding," Thomas said.

Kelly looked at Thomas, then back at Emily, who was floating above the assembled crowd. Emily's reflection showed in Thomas's eyes as he watched in awe.

The man with the flame tattoo on his neck and scar on his face jolted out of a deep sleep, seeing the vision of the Switch family. He quickly got out of bed bearing a blood thirsty expression. He could barely contain himself as he paced the floor.

Kelly and Thomas watched, stunned, until Thomas lost his footing and cracked a small branch.

Brenda turned around. This broke the Switch family's concentration, causing Emily to fall to the ground.

"Brenda, what are you doing?" Carrie said, baffled.

Brenda didn't respond—she just stared at the spot where she heard the noise come from.

"Somebody's over there," Brenda said. It was too dark to see anything.

Emily sat up, exhausted and delirious. Everyone else focused on the bushes that Brenda was staring at. Some of the family picked up their candles. No one could see anything, so they all approached carefully.

Kelly and Thomas were crouched behind the bushes, frozen. The entire Switch family was steadily approaching. The candles illuminating their path with each step. In less than a minute the family was standing right over them. Kelly and Thomas stayed hunched behind the bushes, paralyzed with fear. They thought that their hearts were going to come out of their throats.

Chapter 10

K elly and Thomas felt the chill of the air and the Switch family looming above them. Linda pulled back the bushes and her jaw dropped as she saw the two of them hiding.

"Kelly, what are you doing out here!" Linda said.

Kelly was slow to respond, scared of her own mother. She looked at Linda and the other family members.

"Kelly!" Linda shouted.

Kelly snapped out of her trance.

"What?" she responded weakly.

"What did you see?" Linda asked in a panic.

"Oh, my goodness. They saw everything," Carrie said, her nerves getting the best of her. Carrie put her hands over her face in disbelief that they were so careless. She knew the consequences.

"Kelly, what did you see?" Linda asked again.

"Everything. Who are you?" Kelly said feeling the sting of betrayal and nerves throughout her whole body.

"And she brought the neighbor. What's your name again?" Brenda asked Kelly's new friend.

"Thomas," he stammered.

"Girls. They know," Dorothy said to the rest of her family, seeing through the eyes of a witch hunter who was watching them congregate at that very moment. Then Dorothy's vision slowly faded away.

"Know what?" Kelly asked.

"They're coming, we have to go," Dorothy said.

"Who's coming?" Thomas said.

"Are you guys witches?" Kelly asked.

"We'll talk about it later," Linda said.

"Just answer me!"

"Yes. We are... witches," Linda said, heartbroken, seeing the pain in Kelly's eyes.

"That's why you never talked about your family," Kelly said, putting together a lifetime of lies. Linda sighed, hating to be in this predicament.

"I just wanted you guys to have a normal life," Linda said looking deep into Kelly's eyes.

"But you're not normal. You're chanting in the woods, making Emily fly..."

"Levitate," Brenda chimed in.

"We have to go!" Dorothy said, looking around as if something could jump out of the woods at any moment.

"Who's coming?" Kelly asked once again.

"The witch hunters. Through the eyes of a mortal, when more than three witches are performing a ritual, they can see us, and track us," Dorothy said, being as clear as possible that they were indeed endangered.

"Are you serious?" Thomas said.

"Being they just made my sister hover in the air like a Frisbee, I'm inclined to believe them," Kelly said.

"Kelly, I'm so sorry you had to find out like this," Linda said.

"So Emily's a witch, too?" Kelly asked. Linda hesitated before answering.

"Yes. I knew I was going to have to tell you about my family one day. I just always dreaded it. And you both just grew up so fast."

"Linda, we have to go. Thanks to their little mortal eyes we have to get the heck out of here," Carrie said. Uncle Ray picked up a weak Emily.

"What about Thomas? Will someone come after him?" Kelly asked.

"He'll be fine, they only want witches," Brenda said. Linda reached her hand out for Kelly, but she didn't accept it. Linda grabbed her hand and pulled her along. The rest of the family quickly grabbed the remainder of their things and all headed back as well.

They hustled through the woods as fast as they could. Emily bounced up and down on Uncle Ray's back. Uncle Ray moved really well for a man in his mid-fifties.

Emily tapped him on his shoulder and told him that she might be strong enough to run now. He told her to relax and enjoy the ride. She held him tight.

Emily made eye contact with Kelly as they zigzagged through the brush. She felt terrible about not being able to tell her any of this. She knew Kelly was devastated, just as she was when she first learned their family secret. However, at least she knew what was going on once things started happening.

Kelly was more scared now by her family's reaction to the witch hunters than the fact that they were a family of witches. She thought to herself, what the heck was a witch hunter? Were they killers? Would they expose her family? How dangerous could they be? After all, we're not living in a time of burning witches at the stake. She wondered how many people actually knew about this world of witches. Most of the people who claimed to be witches were really just fans of the culture and the practice of it. Like a religion. They had no real powers and there was nothing supernatural about them. Just faith.

When the family got back to the house, they rushed inside and packed their things as if they had practiced this many times. A kind of Armageddon drill for witches.

Kelly and Emily stood confused, watching family members quickly gather their things. The twins had fear in their eyes. Shonda shot Kelly an evil glare.

"I can't believe we have to leave our home because of her. She's not even in our family," Shonda said, irate.

"Excuse me?" Kelly said, throwing a cold stare of her own.

"You heard me," Shonda replied.

Emily stepped up to Shonda. "She's part of my family. Maybe not yours, but she's part of mine," Emily said, eyes narrowed.

"Whatever. This just sucks. I have a life here and it's gone, just like that," Shonda said.

"Come on, Shonda, that's enough," Rhonda said as she pulled her sister away.

Kelly and Emily went to their room and stared out the window. Linda walked in.

"Make sure you use the bathroom before we leave," she said.

Kelly and Emily watched the rest of the family load their cars.

"This is ridiculous. Is this real?" Kelly said.

"It seems a little overboard to me," Emily said, overwhelmed as well. Linda walked up behind them.

"Well it's not, believe me," Linda said, looking out the window as well. The girls looked at their mother.

"Come on, let's go," Linda said.

The family headed out of the house. Other family members pulled up in their cars. Shonda and Rhonda explained to family members who were not there what happened, pointing at Kelly by the car. Kelly saw them pointing as she put luggage in her mother's car's trunk.

There were three cars and four SUVs loaded up, ready to hit the road. Some of these people Kelly and Emily had never met. Uncle Ray came out with his bags.

Brenda headed to Linda's car.

"I'm riding with Linda and the girls," she said to Carrie.

"Fine, let's go. Uncle Ray, you riding with me?" Carrie asked.

"Whatever's clever," Uncle Ray replied as he hurried over to Carrie's SUV.

Kelly looked across the street at Thomas, sitting on his front porch watching the spectacle. Thomas got up and headed across the street. Kelly met him at the curb.

"Hey," Thomas said.

"Hey," Kelly replied.

"So you guys are leaving, just like that?"

"I guess so," Kelly replied.

"Well, my dad works all of the time, so if you need a place to stay, you're welcome."

"Thanks, but I have to go with my family... Are you going to call me?"

"Of course."

"Well, once again, thanks," Kelly said.

"I got you." He smiled.

"You got me?" She flirted with a smile of her own.

"Yeah, as in got your back." He pulled her to him and kissed her. Emily and Linda watched from their car. As Kelly and Thomas lips parted, they stared into each other's eyes, dazed.

"Kelly, we gotta go!" Linda shouted.

Kelly smiled at Thomas. "Call me," she said. Thomas nodded, totally smitten. Kelly turned and walked over to Linda, Brenda and Emily.

Carrie waited for Dorothy. "Mom, let's go." Dorothy walked out of the house like something was bothering her. She had a broom in her hand, sweeping some dirt off the bottom step. "Mom! What are you doing?" Carrie exclaimed.

"Getting all of this dirt off my porch. Baby, I'm staying here," Dorothy said matter-of-factly.

"What are you talking about?" Carrie said. The rest of the family stopped.

Dorothy sighed.

"I need to stay here. I don't know why, but I do."

"Mom, get in the car," Carrie said as if she was the mother and Dorothy the child.

"Yeah, come on," Brenda reiterated. Dorothy shook her head no.

"Mom, don't," Linda added.

"No, girls. You go. And be safe. If it's my time, it's my time. But my spirit is telling me to stay. We all have our gifts and my spirit is telling me to stay. I think it'll be better for all of us."

"Mom, what do you see?" Carrie asked.

"Sweetie, that's for me and me alone. Now go," Dorothy said in a stern tone. "All of you."

Her daughters were overwhelmed with sadness. Carrie hugged her mother. Then Linda and Brenda hugged Dorothy as well.

"Now you girls go on. Trust me," Dorothy said with conviction.

Linda pulled her mother to the side, away from everyone.

"Mom, please come with us. Whether you had a vision or not. I miss you."

"I miss you, too."

"Well then, come with us."

"I can't. Now you go and do what's best for *your* girls and go on without me."

Linda could see in her mother's eyes there was no convincing her. She sighed and hugged her mother again. She knew her mother had her reasons. Most likely it was to save someone in the family. Maybe her whole family. Her mother gave her a sweet kiss on the lips.

"It's okay. Now go," Dorothy said.

The Switch family got in their cars and caravanned off. Brenda and the girls all looked through the rear window at Dorothy and Thomas standing in the middle of the street watching them drive away. Linda caught a final glimpse of her mother in her rearview mirror as she turned the corner.

Chapter 11

S even vehicles made their way down a long road. It was dark and raining hard. The rain bounced off the concrete, creating a misty fog, making it hard to see. Linda drove with Brenda in the passenger seat. Linda checked her girls in the rearview mirror. The girls stared out of the window, bewildered and depressed. Kelly made eye contact with her mother. Linda felt an incredible amount of guilt. She had wanted to tell her about her family's secret, but felt her curiosity would make Kelly do exactly what she did. Investigate. And see something she was not supposed to see—and she knew the danger of that. So before she spoke she chose her words carefully, trying to express clearly what she was thinking and why she handled things the way she did.

"Kelly, baby, are you okay?" Linda asked.

"I'm fine," Kelly said, continuing to look out her window. She felt like she was in a dream. A kind of romance slash horror movie that she couldn't wake up from. Kelly pinched her forearm, thinking maybe the pain wouldn't hurt, and that she would know she was sleeping peacefully in her bed back in California. And that maybe when she woke up, her father would be there to greet her. But there was pain. And she was still in this bad supernatural horror film where people were trying to kill them. She sighed once again in disbelief.

"Kelly, I am so sorry about all of this," Linda said, sensing her pain and feeling of betrayal.

Kelly rolled her eyes before she replied. "I feel like I'm cursed. First dad, now this," she said, not sure about anything anymore.

"None of this is your fault. I told you, your dad was a freak accident. And this whole thing was just my fault. I should have told you," Linda said.

"Yeah, you should have," Kelly said, matter-of-factly, no fight left in her.

"No, you shouldn't have. It's against witches' law to talk about anything witch related to someone who's not a witch," Brenda said.

"I wanted to tell you..." Emily chimed in. "It was just... that it would have put you at risk. At least that's what they all told me."

"I was going to tell you sooner or later. I just wanted to wait until it was safe," Linda said. "And so your curiosity wouldn't get us in this very predicament."

"Well, being that we are on the run right now, I can see your point," Kelly said.

"I love you, sweetheart, more than anything."

"I love you, too," Kelly said. She looked at her mother in the rearview, then at Emily. The sisters smiled. Brenda smiled as well, first at Kelly and then Linda.

"So you guys are just witches. Not devil worshippers—"

"Oh, God, no!" Linda said. Linda and Brenda shared a laugh.

"Well, thank God. 'Cause I really do have plans on going to heaven," Kelly said.

"You think I don't?" Emily added.

"I don't know. You sneaking around in the night, chanting in the woods, levitating," Kelly said.

Linda chimed in. "It's not what it seems. It's belonging to a special craft of people that are in touch with other dimensions, to be able to make things move, see things that others can't see. Use parts of the brain that others will never be able to use. This is a very rare power that has been in our family for more than five generations," Linda said, looking at Brenda and her two girls in the rearview. "When we chant, we chant from a place of love. And nothing else."

"So what's the difference between this family and all of the other people out there practicing witchcraft?" Kelly asked.

Brenda chimed in. "Well, for starters, they're practicing the craft... and we *are the craft*," she said.

"Nothing's wrong with practicing the craft. It's like praying," Linda said, tightening her grip on the steering wheel, focused on the wet road. "Now what you decide to pray to... that's completely on you. Some pray for goodness and love... and some for evil," Linda said, eyes in the rearview mirror, making sure both girls paid attention.

Brenda chimed back in. "Witchcraft hasn't always had a bad rap. There was a time when to be a witch was just to be a healer, or free thinker. Someone who helped you get closer to whatever God you prayed to," Brenda said, loving to talk about the history of witches and witchcraft. "We call ourselves *true witches* because we are *true* to the telekinetic power we can harness, and to our obligation to never abuse it and always walk in our own truth. We call the witch hunters with the gift of sight *true*, too, because they operate in their own truth as well. But witches who worship anything evil, we call *non-true witches,* whether they have telekinetic power or not."

"So if a witch with no telekinetic power practices witchcraft for good, they're considered a *true witch,* too?" Kelly asked.

"Of course," Linda replied.

"So what do they think of us?" Emily asked.

"They don't *truly* know our kind exist. All they have are rumors, but no proof. If they did, they'd probably call us freak witches. Who knows?" They all laughed. "Nevertheless, we still have a beautiful connection with them."

"Well, like I said, I'm just glad to hear my family isn't a bunch of devil worshippers," Kelly said. Linda and her sister laughed.

"Yeah, I should have just told you what was going on with your sister," Linda said, looking at it from Kelly's point of view. Kelly and her mother shared a slight smile in the rearview.

"It's okay, mom. It's just a lot to take in," Kelly said.

"Yeah, I wish you would have given me a warning as well," Emily said. They all gave a little laugh, amused by Emily's sardonic way.

The seven cars caravanned down the road, Linda's car the last in line. Carrie drove in front of her. Suddenly, all but Carrie's and Linda's cars left the highway. Linda and Brenda looked at each other.

"I guess our escort from the family is over," Linda said.

"Yeah, we're on our own," Brenda said. She turned around making sure the road was clear behind them. "I better call Carrie."

Brenda dialed Carrie. She picked up. "Hey."

"Well, it's just us now. So we're going to hang back, keep a nice distance between us, okay?"

"Sure. Good thinking," Carrie said, speeding up. "Oh, by the way, we're going to get a little help from the Woody family. They heard what happened and want to help."

"Woody family? Who talked to them?" Brenda asked.

"One of the cousins told them what was going on and they said they wanted to help. I told them it wasn't necessary," Carrie said, knowing they could use all the help they could get if things went bad.

"So Larry's coming?"

"No. His sons. Taylor and Zach."

"Why? They're just kids," Brenda said.

"I don't know. Larry said they could be helpful. Maybe once we get there he'll come."

"All right, let's pick up the pace," Brenda said, and hung up.

Their cars sped down the highway.

Linda looked at Brenda. "To the Woody's?" she asked, having heard the conversation.

"That's what Carrie said."

"Larry was always sweet. I haven't seen him in years," Linda said.

"Yeah, it's been a while."

Linda thought about her years as a kid, playing on the Woody ranch. Her father, Stan, and Larry were close friends. They met in the army and discovered they had something in common. A family secret of sorts. They were both from a family of witches. They eventually served together in Vietnam. After the war they traveled the world together before going back home so Stan could marry his long-time sweetheart, Dorothy. He always knew that the two of them would be betroth. Not just because Dorothy was from a family of witches as well, but also because he truly loved her.

Eleven years after they were married, he was killed by a group of witch hunters, leaving Dorothy a widow and Linda and her sisters fatherless. The incident was one of the main reasons Linda wanted to run away when she fell in love with Victor, who was not a witch. It was her opportunity for a normal life, or so she thought. And a fifty-fifty chance that the children she gave birth to would not have the witch trait.

She shook her head at the irony of their current predicament.

The rain finally stopped and the sun woke up. Carrie had driven far up ahead, not wanting to draw attention to them—separating their auras to make it more difficult to be tracked. The highway is always one of the most dangerous places for a coven of witches. It puts them out in the open, exposing them to true witch hunters, who can sense them on the road. But with a witch hunter's trace on them, they had to get as far as they could from the Switch family's home.

Brenda kept her distance from Carrie's car, while Linda slept in the passenger seat. The girls were asleep in the back seat as well. When Carrie finally slowed down, Brenda followed her off the highway and down some back country roads. They pulled up to an archway with a sign that read *Woody's Ranch*. They continued down the long winding dirt road, flanked by cattle all over. After a minute, they came to a big ranch-style home. It had a detached stable a little over a hundred yards away with farm animals all around it.

As they stopped in front of the house, Larry Woody ambled out, supporting himself with a cane. He had a wiry frame and broad shoulders. His hair was all white and he had a long beard. He smiled at the sight of them. Three girls quickly followed him. They were nine, seven, and four. They chased each other around, throwing a ball. An old woman sat on the porch in a rocking chair. She held a cane in one hand and a glass of lemonade in the other.

"Look who's here! I can't believe it!" Larry said in a scruffy voice.

Linda and the girls all woke up. Kelly and Emily watched Larry approach. They looked at each other and shrugged, not knowing what was going on. Linda smiled, not recognizing the man approaching.

"Is that Larry?" Linda said, so only Brenda could hear.

"I think it is," Brenda answered, unsure herself.

"Wow. Has it been that long?" Linda asked.

"I guess it has," Brenda replied as they all got out of their cars.

Carrie, Uncle Ray, and the twins all hugged Larry.

"How you guys doing? It's been so long!" Larry said.

"Look at you, you old dog," Uncle Ray said. The men shook hands for good measure.

"And look at you, Carrie. You look as beautiful as ever. And so do your girls, Brenda." He hugged Brenda. "And Linda, it's been too long."

He hugged Linda, then Kelly and Emily. The girls looked at each other, amused.

"And these must be your girls," he said to Linda, smiling, happy to have some company. He was happy to see his oldest and closest friends once again.

He told them he heard that they had been sighted and were coming his way. And when his boys heard the news, they wanted to help. He said they were young and full of energy and had to grow up sometime.

Linda didn't understand why they were picking up some young kids. She had heard from her mother when they caught up that Larry had two young boys around ten or twelve. She thought maybe they had powers like her mother and were clairvoyant, and could be helpful by just telling if danger approached. Or maybe Larry would just say what the heck and join us on our road trip. But he looked old and frail, not in a position to go anywhere, let alone fight any witch hunters if they had to.

"Here my boys come now," Larry said, pointing to the field. The two boys raced to the house on horseback.

"They're riding fast for some little boys," Linda said.

"Oh, they ain't so little no more," Larry said with a laugh. Linda watched the boys ride toward them, getting older and bigger as they got closer.

As the boys rode up to them, they were all smiles. Both were at least six five, handsome and buff, and shirtless. Their blue eyes showed the witch trait in their pupils and iris.

"They got big!" Carrie said to Larry.

"You think?" Brenda said, amused. The boys had to be between sixteen and eighteen, and had the physiques of gladiators.

"Taylor, Zach, you remember the Switch family?" Larry said.

"Sure. But it's been awhile," Zach, the younger brother respectfully said.

"Hey, boys!" Carrie said.

"Hey," the boys replied. They hopped off their horses, bodies glistening with sweat. Zach did a double-take at Emily. They shared a smile.

"Good to see you guys," Taylor said with a cocky expression. "So, are we going to kick some witch hunter butt?" Zach looked at his older brother as if he had no home training.

They all shook the boys' hands, happy to see them.

Emily and Kelly stood there with their mouths wide open, staring at the boys chest and arms.

"Please tell me, they're not our cousins," Emily said to Kelly so only she could hear. Shonda and Rhonda overheard her.

"They're not," the twins said in unison, staring at the handsome, buff, shirtless brothers, liking what they saw as well. Zach and Emily smiled at each other again.

Larry ushered everyone out back. He had prepared a huge spread. Barbeque was his specialty. They sat at a long table with three bonfires lighting up the backyard. Other members of the Woody family were out back as well.

"I was just so happy to hear from your cousins, then Dorothy. She is such a sweet woman. She asked if I could help. But she knows I'd do anything for her family."

"Thanks, Larry," Carrie said.

"Our kind have to stick together. It's not every day true witches have a bond like our families do."

They all smiled in agreement.

"Your place is so beautiful," Brenda said.

"Yeah, I can remember my dad bringing us here as kids. We used to just play all night," Linda said, with a smile on her face.

"Good times," Larry said.

Linda sat there eating, enjoying seeing her sisters and other members of the Woody family talking. She'd forgotten how wonderful it is to be around people who had the same gifts.

"Hey, you guys want to see something cool?" Zach asked the girls and the twins.

"Sure," Emily said.

Emily looked at Kelly, who shook her head as if Emily was being too easy. Emily shrugged and rolled her eyes as she got up. Kelly laughed, and she and the twins got up as well.

They all headed down to the barn.

"A barn," Rhonda said with a mocking smile.

"Great. We're going to see their favorite pig," Shonda said sarcastic.

Kelly and Emily followed, curious.

"I'm so not milking anything, though," Kelly said.

"If Zach asks me to, I will," Emily said with a chuckle.

"He is cute," Kelly said.

"Fine. You mean fine!"

"Fine. I stand corrected," Kelly said. The girls could not get over how good looking the boys were. Handsome was definitely an understatement when it came to the two young men who towered over them.

Taylor bent over to grab a key under a rock by the barn door.

"Could you guys close your mouth? You're going to drool on the cows," Shonda said so only the girls could hear.

"Our older brother designed it," Taylor said.

"Older brother?" all of the girls asked, their interest piqued.

"Yeah," Taylor said.

"How many brothers you guys got?" Rhonda asked.

"Three more," Zach said matter-of-factly. "You think we're big, wait 'til you see them."

"Where are they?" Shonda asked.

"Yeah, where are they?" Rhonda said, with a curious smile sounding a little too eager.

"Traveling, seeing the world," Zach said.

"Yeah. When they come back, then it'll be our turn," Taylor said.

"Cool," Emily said, transfixed by Zach's smile.

"I can't wait," Zach said, lighting up at the thought of an adventure overseas. "Maybe you guys will come with us," Zach flirted.

The girls looked at each other with smiles. The twins smiled as well, thinking they could have a shot with one of the three older brothers.

They entered the barn, which was so dark they couldn't see their own hand in front of their face if they tried. Taylor flicked on the light switch. The barn lit up, resembling the inside of a fabulous circus tent. There were high wires and trampolines. They also had a trapeze with a net underneath. There was also an extremely daunting obstacle course, with walls, ropes, tires, sand pits, and monkey bars, that took up the entire barn. Kelly and Emily walked by a host of exercise equipment. There was a weight bench with at least five hundred pounds on the bar. Emily nudged Kelly and nodded at the bar, impressed.

"How much do *you* weigh?" Kelly said to Emily. Emily laughed.

"Whatever I weigh, it seems as though he can handle it," Emily said with a grand smile. Kelly laughed at the thought of them being bad.

The twins scanned the barn looking at the incredible contraptions. The Woody brothers looked at the twins and smiled, proud of their extravaganza of a barn. The twins couldn't help but be impressed, wanting to play, while Kelly and Emily were in agreement that they were going to just sit back and watch. And watch they did, as the twins and Woody brothers ran and jumped, flipped, and flew through the air with the reflexes of cats.

The other Switch family members wanted to make sure the three sisters and their kids got out of the state safely before they doubled back and went home. Dorothy assured them if they were out of the state they had a better chance of not encountering any witch hunters. But just in case the witch hunters were closer than they thought, they would have a little backup. They knew it was never good for too many witches to travel together on the open road. Besides, only Uncle Ray, Carrie, Brenda, Linda, Shonda, Rhonda, and Emily were in danger. The other Switch family members and even Kelly and Thomas were not. But anything was possible when it came to witch hunters. Some were wild and marched to their own beat. These were witch hunters without code—the ones who if they sighted you would track you to the end of the earth and do anything to kill you. Even kill humans if they got in their way. But typically witch hunters only had forty-eight hours to track a witch they sighted; otherwise, chances of them catching and killing them would be lost forever. So witches would flee—and the witch hunters would pursue them—with the utmost urgency.

But what Dorothy didn't tell any of her family members was that she knew who was in the most danger. The person who had the biggest chance of being killed by the witch hunters. The person she saw in a vision appear to die. That person was her. She knew they were coming and coming soon. And being the oldest, she was their priority target. She was like a beacon to the witch hunter who sighted them, so she had to stay back—and most of all away from her loved ones. She didn't want anything to happen to her family and she knew her family would not leave if they knew she was the main target. This was her way of protecting them.

However, a witch alert over the radio, telling all witch hunters to look out for them, did not make things easy for them. Which is exactly why there were three brand new black SUVs coming up fast from behind.

Chapter 12

T he black trucks caught Brenda's attention in the rearview mirror. Her stomach dropped. She tapped Linda in the passenger seat. Even though Brenda's heart was racing she seemed calm and cool. Linda stirred awake. Brenda gave her a look that said things were *not okay*. Linda rubbed her face, waking herself up. She turned around and saw the SUVs approaching. Linda looked at her sister, then at the girls sound asleep in the back seat.

"Girls," Linda said, tapping their legs. Kelly and Emily woke up to their mother's nervous expression. They were instantly concerned. They followed their mother's eyes behind them and saw the black SUVs riding their bumper.

Fear spread across Emily's and Kelly's faces. "Are these witch hunters?" Emily asked.

"Not sure," Linda said.

"But most likely," Brenda added.

"Mom, they're going to hit us," Kelly said in fear.

"Calm down, Kelly," Linda said, then looked back at Brenda. "Brenda…"

"I'm already ahead of you." Brenda punched the pedal to the floor.

They sped down the road at almost ninety miles an hour. Brenda gave Linda a look. Linda nodded.

Linda stared at the black SUV on their bumper. She looked at Brenda, who nodded for her to do what she could. Linda held the palms of her hands out toward the SUV. Suddenly a purple light shot out of her hands, and blew out the tires on the first SUV. It swerved, barely maintaining control as it pulled over to the side. She did the same thing to the second and third SUVs. Kelly and Emily looked at Linda amazed.

"They're amateurs. Contract players," Brenda said.

"How did you do that?" Kelly asked.

"It's a gift," Linda winked.

"Can you do that, too?" Kelly asked Brenda.

"Yep, your mother taught me," Brenda said. "I'm glad you didn't lose your touch," Brenda said to Linda.

"It's like riding a bike," Linda said. "I was just trying not to flip them on accident. I'd hate to kill someone for just being stupid followers."

"You guys are freaking me out," Kelly said.

"Yeah, me too," Emily added. Kelly looked at Emily oddly.

"What else can you do?" Kelly asked her mother.

"We can move things. Manipulate time and space. Move air."

Kelly thought about her dad and the accident. Linda saw the look in her eyes.

"What's wrong?" Linda asked.

"So you catching me that day wasn't a freak accident?"

Linda didn't say anything at first, but then she exhaled. "No it wasn't, sweetie."

"And you picked me?" Kelly asked. Linda hesitated before answering.

"Yes," Linda said with loving eyes. "I did what any mother would have done… or father." Kelly's eyes welled up but before a tear could roll down her cheek she wiped the corners of her eyes. Emily put her arm around her.

Brenda hung up her cell phone.

"Carrie's not answering," Brenda said, a little concerned.

"What do you think?" Linda said, concerned as well.

"I'll catch up with them."

They sped down the highway until they finally pulled up next to Carrie's SUV. Everyone was packed inside. The Woody brothers were in the very back seat, crammed in the third row. They looked like giants, rocking their heads back and forth to the rock music blasting in the car. The twins enjoyed the music as well, singing along. Carrie had on earmuffs, obviously not liking the music. Linda, Brenda, and the girls looked at the boys singing wildly to music, beating their hands on the seats in front of them.

Chapter 13

A white Hummer pulled up, with a Jeep and mobile home following it. Gimon got out of the Hummer, accompanied by his three henchmen, Stem, Mason, and Cam.

Cam started to pump gas while Gimon pulled out a big cigar and smoked. "We're getting close," Gimon said. He texted alerts to his network of witch hunters, feeding them information on what he thought the witches were driving and what they might look like.

"Did you call our boys in North Carolina?" Mason asked.

"Yeah, but I don't expect much out of them," Gimon said.

"This is huge. We haven't tracked a master family in what?" Cam asked.

"Twenty-three years. Since my father used to take me hunting," Gimon said.

"Are they aware?" Mason asked.

"Of course they are. We'll be able to track them better the closer we get," Gimon said as he blew out a puff of smoke.

A gas station attendant walked up to Gimon, trying to be as nice as possible but daunted by the group of witch hunters.

"Excuse me, sir, there's no smoking… with the gas and all."

Gimon gave him a baleful look. He grabbed the guy by the collar and put out the cigar on his forehead. The attendant screamed and ran off.

"I'm not one to break the rules," Gimon said. They all laughed. Gimon's laughter slowly came to a halt as he took in the fresh air. He closed his eyes, having a sighting.

"You sense something, boss?" Mason asked.

"Something. But not who we're looking for."

"Are they close?" Cam asked.

Gimon smiled. "Oh yeah. Boys, we're going to take a little detour before we catch up with the others," he said as his face turned serious. They all got in their vehicles and drove off.

Linda drove with the girls in the back seat. Kelly was on her cell phone talking to Thomas. Brenda showed Emily how to levitate a pen. Kelly shook her head, amazed by her new predicament as she watched an airborne pen rock back and forth.

"Everything okay?" Thomas asked, laying on his sofa next to the living room window.

"Yeah, everything's fine. They're not devil worshippers," Kelly said playfully.

The ladies in the car gave a little laugh.

"Well that's good," Thomas said. Kelly shot her mother a smile in the mirror. "I think I miss you already," she whispered.

"I think I miss you too," Thomas said, beaming. He said to himself, that he had never missed any girl before.

"I think I'll be able to come visit you after a few weeks, once things settle down. My mom said the family will just have to move out of the neighborhood, but we'll definitely move back."

"Well, I do have a car."

"So you'll drive and come see me?"

"Of course," he said with a smile.

"Good," Kelly said flirting over the phone in her own world. When she looked up, everyone in the car was staring at her. They laughed. "Can you guys get out of my conversation?" she said playfully. They all continued to laugh.

Thomas smiled at the laughter on the other end of the phone. His eyes drifted outside his window across the street. "Who the heck is that?" Thomas said.

"Huh?" Kelly said. "Who? You talking to me?" she asked.

"At your grandmother's house. Some guys are on her porch." Thomas stood up to get a better look. He peered out of the window. "And they're all in black and wearing combat boots!"

"There's someone at the house," Kelly announced? Everyone looked at Kelly, concerned.

"They're looking through the windows," Thomas said, watching the people in black.

"He said they're looking through your mom's window," Kelly said. Linda and Brenda looked at each other worried, feeling powerless at being so far away.

Thomas stared at the people looking around the house. One of them turned around to survey the neighborhood, and Thomas backed out of sight. Then he peeked through the window, hiding behind curtains that were halfway drawn. The man in black caught the eye of Thomas staring through his window. Thomas quickly moved back and closed the curtains. He stood frozen, thinking of his next move.

"Kelly, they saw me," Thomas whispered into the phone. He started to pace.

Suddenly there was a hard knock on the door. Thomas stopped in his tracks.

"They're knocking," Thomas said calmly, staying still.

The knocks came harder and harder, to the point of shaking the whole house.

"They're not leaving," Thomas said, remaining cool.

Kelly listened closely on the phone, terrified for him. "Thomas, get out of there," she said.

Thomas stood frozen, his back up against the wall where no one could see him from outside.

"They're kicking my door," he whispered into the phone.

"Run! Run, Thomas!" Kelly screamed.

"Get away from my door!" Kelly heard Thomas yell. She then heard the door crash down, and a scuffle. The phone went dead.

"Oh my God, oh my God! Turn around, mom!" Kelly banged on the back of the car seat. Emily rubbed Kelly's back trying her best to comfort her.

"Kelly, calm down! Calm down!" Linda shouted.

"Stop the car!" Kelly screamed. Linda pulled the car over to the side of the road.

Kelly jumped out of the car, crying hysterically. Linda went after her. She caught up to her and held her while she cried in her arms. Brenda and Emily sat in the car, watching.

"I'm so sorry," Linda said. "This is the ugly part of my world that I never wanted you to see. I'm sorry."

Linda held Kelly tight as she wept uncontrollably.

After Linda ushered Kelly back to the car, the four of them followed Carrie's car down the dark road. Kelly tried to call Thomas again. No response.

"I'm sure he got away. You did tell him to run," Emily said, trying to reassure her sister. Kelly nodded, hoping she was right.

They were all quiet except Brenda, who was talking to Carrie on the phone. Carrie rode with her twins and the Woody brothers. Carrie's car was silent as well, as everyone listened to her conversation with Brenda.

"Let's just hope that mom wasn't home," Carrie said, seeing them following way behind in the rearview mirror.

"Well, if she was hurt, we'd have felt it, right?" Brenda asked.

"Yeah. Look, let's keep even more distance between us, just to be safe," Carrie said, concerned, looking at the big Woody brothers in the back seat. "Nine witches traveling on a practically empty highway, we might as well paint a bullseye on our cars."

"Okay."

"I'll call you back," Carrie said.

"All right," Brenda replied and hung up. "Carrie said we should lay back even more."

"Okay," Linda said as she slowed down to let Carrie get farther ahead. She crept along in the slow lane while cars zipped pass them.

As soon as Carrie hung up, the twins started to ask questions.

"What happened, mom?" Shonda asked.

"Some witch hunters came by the house."

"Was grandma there?"

"I don't think so. Brenda talked to some of the cousins. They said they were going to go get her and take her to their house whether she wanted to go or not."

"So she's okay?" Rhonda said.

"Yes."

"You sure?" Shonda said, wanting her mother to do a better job reassuring them.

"She's okay, I would have felt something if she wasn't," Carrie said.

"Witch hunters are so stupid. Grandma's too smart for them anyway," Shonda said.

"I heard stories about your grandmother. She was a very strong witch in her day," Zach said to the twins.

"She still is, Zach," Carrie said.

"So we shouldn't worry about it?" Shonda said.

"No. She's just fine. Most of us Switch family members can feel when one of us is in a terrible amount of pain. No matter how far away she is. That's how we knew that something was wrong with my sister Linda when her husband died. We all felt it... I just can't imagine how those kids feel," Carrie said, somber.

The twins looked at each other, knowing the hard time they've been giving both of the girls. They continued to ride in silence. Carrie smiled, trying to break the tension.

"So, boys, how's your dad doing these days?" Carrie asked.

"He's good. He just watches TV most of the time," Taylor said.

"He can't get enough of the soaps," Zach added.

"Shood, you can't get enough of the soaps either," Taylor said, laughing.

"I just watch because dad watches."

"No you don't, you watch because you love it. Zach's a romantic. He's always getting his heart broke by some girl."

The twins looked at Zach, sympathetic.

"Oh, we're going there?" Zach replied with an embarrassed look. Taylor laughed.

"What's the name of that last girl that dumped you?" Taylor asked, undaunted by Zach's now-threatening eyes.

Zach sighed.

"Sophie. And for your info she didn't dump me, the split was mutual," Zach said with a sardonic smile.

"My brother's too much of a nice guy to break up with a girl. She dumped him."

"Well maybe she didn't know a good thing when she saw it," Shonda said.

"Yeah, you're a good-looking guy, Zach. Forget her," Rhonda said, flirting.

Taylor smiled, amused at Rhonda's flirtation. Shonda smiled as well at Rhonda's boldness.

Zach sensed that Rhonda liked him. He smiled, even though neither of the twins was his type. His type was more like Emily.

"I'm taking a little break from women," Zach said with a deep sigh. "It's too much work."

"It doesn't have to be," Rhonda said.

"That's what all women say," Taylor chimed in. "You girls say that and then here comes the drama."

"Please. It's boy's that cause the drama," Shonda shot back.

"Are you kidding? You girls never know what you want. You guys always try to control everything," Taylor said.

"That is true, ladies," Zach added.

"You know it," Taylor said.

The brothers gave each other a high-five.

"Well, maybe the ladies can't figure out what they want because the boys are constantly changing their minds and are too immature and want to date everything they see," Shonda said. The girls gave each other their own high-five.

They continued into their fiery debate about boys and girls and the wows of relationships. Carrie shook her head as if they were all stupid.

Gimon, Stem, Cam, and Mason stood in front of a big farm house. "Let's go," Gimon said. They strolled up to the front door. Gimon pulled out his witch detector device, resembling a walkie-talkie. He put it to the door and it made a crackling sound. Gimon smiled. "I told you."

Cam gave a sadistic smile and kicked the front door down. A woman inside screamed. Gimon looked into her eyes as she bolted through the house yelling "Run Jacob.... Run!" Stem ran after her and tackled her in the hallway. Nine-year-old Jacob stood in the kitchen in shock staring back at Gimon. The boy snapped out of his trance and bolted through the house toward the french doors that opened onto the back yard.

The doors flew open without the boy even touching them. He darted out of the house and into the fields. Gimon savored the moment, taking in a deep breath as he stared at his fellow witch hunters, who held the mother down.

Jacob ran through the cornfields, terrified, with Gimon right on his heels. He fell and got up fast, seeing Gimon in pursuit with a sick glare in his eyes and a calm stride. Gimon was very fast for a big man and was quickly gaining on the boy. Gimon reached into his waistband. The boy's petrified adorable face did nothing to slow Gimon as he closed in. A gunshot rang out and black crows flew sporadically up into the sky. The woman in the house cried out with a heart-wrenching scream, knowing that her little boy was dead.

Chapter 14

As sunlight faded into darkness, Kelly, Emily, Brenda, and Linda hiked into the woods. They had parked their cars far off road along with Carrie's SUV, which was hidden under a large tree. They were at least three miles deep in the woods just to be safe, letting their flashlights be their guide to their destination.

"You sure we're going the right way?" Linda asked Brenda, thinking they should have caught up with Carrie and the rest of the family by now.

"Carrie said go to the big tree in front of their car and head east," Brenda said, holding a big bag of food that they had stopped off to get for everyone. They continued to walk farther into the woods. They finally spotted a bonfire, surrounded by Uncle Ray, Carrie, the Woody brothers, and the twins.

They camped out, enjoying the beautiful night and the stars that lit up the sky like a Christmas tree.

"I can't believe we're camping out in the woods," Kelly said to her mother.

"Trust me. If you're ever in danger, the woods is the safest place for a witch," Linda said.

"Hey ladies, here's some more to drink," Carrie said, placing a liter of soda next to them.

The twins walked up to Kelly. "Hey Kelly," Shonda said.

"Hey," Kelly answered, a little apprehensive.

"Look. I'm sorry about being so difficult," Shonda said.

"Yeah, me too. Are we cool?" Rhonda asked with a friendly smile. Kelly looked at Emily, who gave her a smile and a nod.

"Yeah," Kelly said.

"So we're all family?" Shonda said with a friendly smile as she rubbed Kelly's shoulder.

"Of course," Kelly said. The four girls hugged.

Carrie, Linda and Brenda sat by a tent, watching their girls talk becoming friendlier with each other.

Uncle Ray sat in a chair relaxing while the Woody brothers put up another tent, arguing over the best way to do it. The twins, Emily, and Kelly watched them giggling. Zach and Emily made eye contact and smiled at each other.

"And there it is," Kelly said, laughing. "Emily's kind of a boy magnate."

"I'm not thinking about him," Emily said, while throwing smiles Zach's way.

"I saw the way Zach looked at you," Shonda said.

"Second that. I threw him a little action, but he didn't take the bait," Rhonda said. The girls laughed.

"They're both cute," Kelly said.

"Yes they are..." the twins and Emily replied in unison. They all laughed.

Later that night Linda began to teach Emily how to use her powers. Linda sent a shock wave to knock down a water bottle sitting on a branch. Emily couldn't quite get it. Linda explained that Emily needed to be more focused. Emily tried, but could only make the water bottle vibrate. She grew more frustrated.

"Come on, Emily, concentrate," Kelly said.

"I am," Emily said.

"She'll get it," Brenda said. "I was a slow learner, too. Some of us get it slow and some of us fast."

"Linda was a slow learner, too. But once she got it, she got it," Carrie said, impressed with her sister's abilities. "I got it fast," she bragged. Brenda smirked and rolled her eyes at her.

Uncle Ray came up behind Emily and put his hands on her shoulders.

"Come on, child, get out of your head and just make the bottle fall." Uncle Ray held Emily's hand toward the bottle.

"Come on, Emily, become one with the bottle," Shonda added. Emily focused as hard as she could, extending her hand toward the bottle. The bottle moved a little, then fell. They all cheered.

"You did it!" Kelly said as she applauded her sister. Emily looked at her hands stunned, wearing a big smile.

"Wow," Emily said.

"Did you feel it?" Linda asked.

"Yeah. It felt electric," Emily said, still looking at her hands.

"My sister's a true witch," Kelly said with glee. Kelly and Emily hugged, jumping up and down like two schoolgirls playing Double Dutch. The rest of the family continued to applaud amused, seeing the girls celebrating Emily's small victory.

Time passed and darkness continued to own the woods. No moon in sight. Just darkness. And a very small campfire that had been reduced to smoke and ashes.

They slept in sleeping bags under a large canopy. However, Kelly was still up, wrapped in blankets. She rested against a tree, tears in her eyes as she scrolled through pictures of her dad on her cell phone. She thought for a moment, then went to her text messages. To her surprise and delight, the messages from her father were still there. She scrolled through their back-and-fourth conversations. The silly talk that they used during the day. All of their messages ended with a *love you.*

Kelly smiled, wanting to text her father in hopes that he would text her back. She typed *Daddy are you there?* She felt silly doing it, so she deleted it. She knew her father was no longer there, and that she had to talk to him through prayer now. She exhaled.

Linda stirred awake and saw Kelly full of tears. She got up, blankets still wrapped around her, and went to Kelly, knowing that this was all too much for her to handle. Kelly saw her mom approaching and cut her phone off. Linda sat down beside her daughter and put her arm around her. Kelly smiled and wiped her tears, holding her cell phone to her chest.

"Are you okay?" Linda asked.

Kelly nodded and leaned into her mother. "Mom, can we go back and make sure Thomas is okay?" Kelly asked.

"Not now. But later," Linda said.

"I might have got him killed. I'm freaking cursed," Kelly said.

"You're not cursed." Linda rubbed Kelly's back to comfort her.

"I can't stop thinking about dad, and I brought Thomas into all this. And you guys," Kelly said. "None of this is your fault. So stop saying that it is."

"I just wish we could go back in time and fix everything."

"Me too."

"I mean, with all your powers, you can't do anything?"

"I wish I could."

"Maybe we were too happy. And God had to throw drama in the mix to balance it all out?"

"We were happy, weren't we?" Linda said with a smile.

"Yes. Really happy. We had everything."

"But that's what life is. Ups and downs, highs and lows. Misfortune. Maybe this is how we learn and grow as people. Maybe God wants us to develop the resilience to overcome these kinds of adversities."

"Maybe. But it still doesn't seem fair."

"No it doesn't, sweetie."

"I just wish I could tell dad *I love you* one last time."

"He knows you love him."

"You think about him every night, too?" Kelly asked.

"Absolutely."

"But we got each other. And he's with God now."

"Yeah."

"Did I ever tell you how I met your dad?"

"You met him on the bus when you tripped and he helped you up. And it was love at first sight."

"Well, not quite. The first time I met your dad was not quite as simple as that."

Kelly sat up, her interest piqued.

"I was on the bus. But some girls and a couple of boys were teasing me about my outfit. Calling me a witch and a devil worshipper and saying all kinds of crazy stuff."

"Oh my goodness! Did you dress Goth, too?"

"Well, not quite as Goth as the twins, but enough to separate me from the average girl in school. Anyway, to make a long story short. They started pushing me and hitting me. The bus driver did nothing. So I got off the bus, and these girls and boys—who I guess really needed a hug from their parents—kept picking on me. They were just terrible. I knew how to use my powers, but my mom said never to use them on anyone unless it was a matter of life and death. So these girls kept hitting me, and I was trying to get away. Then one of them hit me in the head with a big book bag. I fell and hit my head on the curb. I was out. When I woke up, the girls were helping their boyfriends off of the ground. Victor had jumped on the boys and beat the crap out of them. I looked up and all I saw was his hand, helping me up. He was like an angel. He was like a superhero. So brave. And so full of love. So I'm at peace with him being gone. He would have given his life for any of us without even thinking twice. He was just that kind of man. He loved hard. And when I revealed I was a witch, he just said *I still love you* without a second thought."

"I miss him so much," Kelly said.

"I do, too. We'll get through this. Besides, he's still in here." Linda pointed to Kelly's heart. "Now get some sleep," she said, hugging Kelly for a nice long moment.

"Okay. I'll try."

Linda smiled and went back to her sleeping bag. Kelly looked at her mother, feeling a little better. She then stared up at the heavens and mouthed, *love you.*

The sky continued to get clearer, to the point it made the stars illuminate where it seemed as though you could reach up and grab a star to your liking.

As the rest of the Switch family slept, Kelly remained awake, staring up at the sky. She looked at her mother curled up asleep. She inhaled the fresh air, taking in the beautiful night.

Just as Kelly's eyes finally closed, she heard a sound from the woods. She sat up, looking around. She saw nothing. She looked at her family, all of them still asleep. Then back to the woods. She stared in the direction she thought she heard the sound. But the night was calm and the woods were silent.

Just as she was about to lay back down, she stopped cold at the sight of movement in the brush.

A witch hunter used his hand to signal more witch hunters to follow. They all had shotguns and were dressed in army fatigues.

Kelly watched the witch hunter move closer and closer until their eyes met. Frozen and terrified as more witch hunters came out from behind the trees and brush, the only thing Kelly could hear was her heart beating faster and faster. She trembled with fear, looking at her family lying asleep, unaware of what was happening. Then she looked back at the witch hunters, particularly the one staring directly at her. She tried to say something, anything, but her mouth was not working. Nothing was. But then...

"Hunters!" Kelly screamed, expelling all of the air in her body, sending out a cold fog like a dragon sends a flame.

Everyone in the family jumped up. Linda sent out a purple blast, throwing one of the witch hunters into a tree.

The witch hunters fired their guns. Members of the family took cover behind trees. Linda looked to Kelly and Emily—terrified for her girls.

"Emily, Kelly, run!" Linda yelled.

"Mom..." Emily shouted.

"Go, Emily!" Linda yelled back.

"Come on," Kelly shouted to Emily.

Linda sent out a purple blast, giving her girls an opportunity to run.

Emily and Kelly took off, running deep into the woods away from the gunfire. Two witch hunters fired at them. The Woody brothers delivered a purple blast of their own, knocking the two gunmen into different trees.

Shonda and Rhonda sent a flash, knocking a witch hunter into the dirt. Carrie and Brenda did the same.

A witch hunter got on one knee, firing deep into the woods, barely missing them as Emily and Kelly ran through the brush almost out of sight. Uncle Ray sent a shock wave, knocking him into a tree, then a ditch.

The witch hunter Kelly made eye contact with saw the two sisters run off, but he continued to blast away at the Switch family using trees as shields.

"Carrie, watch out!" Linda shouted. Carrie turned around and blasted a witch hunter into a tree.

A witch hunter aimed at Shonda at close range, then pulled the trigger, but in what seemed like slow motion, Uncle Ray jumped in front of the blast, sacrificing himself. The blast knocked him to the ground, filling his chest with blood.

Everyone was horrified and in disbelief.

Uncle Ray's body slowly evaporated into what looked like glittered ashes, which twirled up into the sky.

Seeing this, the three sisters realized the finality of Uncle Ray and became enraged.

As the hunters continued to fire at them, they snapped out of it and sent purple blasts at anything that moved in the woods.

"No!" the three sisters screamed. The twins seemed out of it, seeing their mother and aunts screaming...

Linda saw a witch hunter aiming at Brenda. "Brenda!" she shouted. Brenda ducked and Linda blasted the witch hunter. Linda ran out in the open like a woman possessed. "Come on, you bastards!"

"No!" Carrie yelled at the witch hunters as she came out from behind a tree and stood next to Linda, sending out her own purple blast.

Brenda took cover, fighting off another group of witch hunters.

Shonda blasted the witch hunter who shot Uncle Ray, killing him instantly. Rhonda blasted him again for good measure.

The Woody brothers sent a powerful blast that knocked down six witch hunters like bowling pins.

Kelly and Emily ran deep through the woods, but were still within earshot of the gunfire. It sounded like a war zone as they ran from the shotgun blasts and the purple flashes that lit up the sky.

"Come on," Kelly said, leading the way.

"Slow down," Emily said.

"Over here," Kelly said.

They hid behind a boulder.

"Let's stay here until mom comes and gets us," Kelly said. They could only sit and listen to the gunfire that echoed through the woods.

"What if she doesn't come?" Emily said.

"She'll come."

They looked at each other, unsure if they would ever see their mother again.

The Switch family continued to fight as the witch hunters scattered and surrounded them. Linda and her sisters looked at each other, knowing this was not looking good for them.

Behind the boulder, deep in the woods, Kelly and Emily waited for their mother. The gunfire eventually stopped. They looked at each other; they did not know what to think. This could have been good or bad.

"What do you think? Should we go back?" Emily asked.

"No. We need to stay here and wait for mom."

Kelly and Emily sat quietly behind the boulder. Kelly broke the silence. "Can you believe this?" she said.

"What, these witch hunters?"

"No, all of it. One minute we're in California, having a normal wonderful life. And now we're out here, hiding in the woods behind a rock. Oh, and you and mom are witches." Emily shot Kelly a look. "What? You guys are witches."

"Whatever."

"It's like a nightmare," Kelly said. Emily looked at her and exhaled while they waited. Ten minutes passed without a gunshot.

"All right, I'm going back," Emily said, looking around the boulder.

Kelly sighed and peeked from behind the huge rock as well. They both saw nothing.

"Are you coming?" Emily said.

"All right. Let's do it," Kelly replied.

They eased up from behind the rock and headed toward the campsite. Kelly and Emily heard something up ahead and froze. They hid as best they could and waited for their mother—or anyone—to call out their names. But no one did.

"Mom, is that you?" Kelly asked, just loud enough for someone close by to hear.

"Mom? Aunt Brenda?" Emily called out a little louder.

Suddenly a branch exploded above them. The familiar witch hunter Kelly saw first, charged them firing a gun that looked more like a cannon.

"Die!" the witch hunter screamed as he ran at them with crazed eyes.

The girls ran as fast as they could.

"Faster, Emily!"

They continued to run, jumping over rocks, branches, and ditches.

Kelly led the way as almost everything around them exploded from gunshots. Kelly jumped over a large broken branch. Emily jumped, but fell. Kelly reeled around, feeling almost out of her own body, seeing Emily's dismal fate.

Kelly saw the witch hunter approach Emily, like a hunter approaches a wounded deer that needs to be put out of its misery. She ran to Emily and tried to help her up. However, by the time Kelly got her to her knees, the crazed witch hunter was standing over them wearing a grim smile, gun drawn. They stared at him, terrified, hands up—surrendering to the gunshot that was soon to come. His eyes told them there was nothing they could do or say to stop him. Emily shot her hand out toward him, eyes closed, focusing with everything she had, only to have an innocuous purple bubble appear out of her hand. The witch hunter jumped at first, but then laughed as the purple bubble slowly floated toward him. He studied it as it glided through the air. He took his index finger and popped it. He laughed even harder. He aimed at Emily, finger on the trigger.

"Babies," the witch hunter said, amused.

Kelly and Emily held each other tight. He pulled the trigger, firing straight at Emily.

Kelly almost simultaneously jumped in front of Emily, sending a red blast at the witch hunter. The witch hunter flew into a tree hard, sending him into a wild spiral before he hit the ground, rendering him dead.

The girls looked at the witch hunter sprawled out on the ground, then at Kelly's hands, stunned. Her hands possessed a red glow that quickly faded. They looked at each other, speechless, then snapped out of their daze on hearing a familiar voice.

"Girls!"

Linda came running, desperately looking for her children. She saw Kelly and Emily on the ground.

"Girls!" Linda shouted. She was relieved to see them alive, having heard the gunshots.

Kelly and Emily jumped up, elated to see their mother. They all hugged.

"Are you okay?" Linda asked, surveying their surroundings and seeing the dead witch hunter's mangled body.

"Yeah," Emily said. Kelly looked down at her hands, feeling the tingling sensation in them.

Linda looked again at the dead witch hunter, then back at Emily. She felt bad that her daughter had to actually kill a witch hunter. She was young and new to this world.

"Emily…" Linda said, empathizing with the pain and confusion she must have felt.

"It wasn't me, Kelly did it. She stopped him," Emily said as she looked at Kelly. Linda's eyes widened, bewildered, not understanding. It made no sense. She thought maybe Kelly used a gun but didn't see anything resembling a weapon around.

"She has powers like us," Emily said.

Linda's eyes fluttered, taking in what Emily was saying.

"How could that be?" Linda said, staring at Kelly in wonderment and confusion.

Kelly stared back at her mother, perplexed herself. She then looked at Emily, who stared at her with excitement in her eyes, happy to be alive and thrilled that Kelly was a witch, too.

"I don't know. Mom…" Kelly said, searching her mother's eyes for an explanation.

"Oh, my goodness," Linda said, as her expression changed, her mind running too fast for her to keep up. She looked deep into Kelly's eyes; her dark brown pupils and iris showed nothing that resembled the traits of a witch. She thought if Kelly's eyes were a lighter color she might have noticed something a long time ago. But Kelly was black and, like most black people, her eyes were dark brown, which meant her witch traits were impossible to detect. She continued to stare at Kelly, looking deep into her eyes, putting the pieces together.

New Orleans on Bourbon Street. Linda and Victor strolled around, pushing eleven-month-old Emily in a stroller. Crowds of people danced and drank, celebrating in the streets. Linda noticed an older black woman watching her from across the boulevard; the woman had seemed to be following her for a few blocks. The woman was dressed in African attire, with a baby secured to her chest in a woven wrap that matched her beautiful dress. Her name was Bendu. She was seventy-seven, with long locks that stretched down to her lower back. There was a mysticism about her.

We were on a family vacation at the jazz festival in New Orleans. An older black woman followed me for blocks," Linda explained to her girls.

Linda breast-fed her baby on a bench on the sidewalk, waiting for Victor to come out of the department store. She smiled lovingly at her baby, then put her back in the stroller and covered it completely with the blanket. Bendu approached her carefully.

"Excuse me, my lady?"

"Yes?" Linda said, taken aback.

"How old is your baby?" Bendu asked.

"Eleven months," Linda replied.

"Can I see her?" Bendu asked.

Linda hesitated, but felt that it was safe to show her Emily being that the woman had her own baby and was obviously a grandmother. "Sure." Linda pulled back the blanket, revealing Emily. The older woman looked and smiled.

"Oh, she is gorgeous. She has beautiful eyes," the woman said, staring at Emily.

"Can I see your baby?" Linda asked.

"Grandbaby. Sure." Bendu unwrapped a chocolate, beautiful baby girl who had to be no more than two months old.

"Oh my goodness. She is adorable," Linda said, falling instantly in love. "Talk about beautiful."

"Thank you," Bendu said.

"My name is Linda."

"My name is Bendu."

"What's her name?" Linda asked.

"Well, she doesn't have one yet."

Linda looked at her, perplexed.

"That will be for the mother to give."

"Where is the mother?" Linda asked, wondering why the old woman was outside with a baby so young. The woman hesitated before answering.

"She passed away."

"Oh, I'm sorry to hear that."

"She passed giving birth."

"Oh my."

"But that's life," Bendu said, at peace with it.

"So, are you just here visiting or do you live here?"

"Visiting."

"How old is she?" Linda asked.

"Two months."

Linda smiled, knowing that was the age that popped in her head. "She is as cute as a button," Linda said, smiling down at her.

"Would you like to hold her?" Bendu asked. Linda was surprised but couldn't resist.

"Sure," Linda replied.

Bendu handed Linda the baby. Linda melted as she held the baby close. The baby looked at her with her big beautiful dark brown eyes and smiled.

"She likes you," Bendu said.

"Well, I like her, too. She is so cute," Linda said, rocking her ever so gently. She stared at the baby in wonderment. Bendu watched, wearing a little smile followed by a hint of sadness.

Linda looked up and saw Victor paying for some snacks inside the store.

"The baby has chosen you," the woman said with a satisfied expression.

"Excuse me?" Linda said.

"Yes. You're the one."

Linda stared at her intensely as the woman took a step back. "Ma'am..." Linda said, baffled by her statement and the fact that she was slowly backing away.

"She has no one else. I would raise her... but I'm very ill and don't have much time left."

"I'm sorry, but I can't..."

"It is you. It is you."

"Ma'am," Linda said, shaken to her core by the woman's action. Linda walked toward the woman, stunned. "Ma'am!"

The woman continued to back away, and suddenly disappeared in the crowd. Linda looked for her but she was gone. Linda made her way through the throng of people in the streets her heart beating twice as fast. Victor walked out of the store and saw that Emily was in her stroller but Linda was walking through the crowd of people in the streets. Leaving Emily alone on the sidewalk.

"Hey, Linda! Where you going?"

He saw that she was holding a little baby wrapped in an African blanket, looking around for someone. She looked at Victor in dismay.

"What you got there?" he asked, confused.

Linda simply stared at him, speechless.

Deep in the woods Linda smiled at the revelation of Kelly being a witch. Kelly looked at her mother, flabbergasted.

Linda shook her head. It was so clear now. She wiped a tear out of her eye before she spoke, amazed at how funny and beautiful life could be.

"She knew what I was. A witch. I always thought that she picked me because I looked like I had a nice family. Or maybe because I could breast feed you and bond with you. Which I did... Then, later, when I found out that I couldn't have any more children, I just thought you were a gift from God. Which you are. But now I know. She knew I was a witch... just like you."

The girls were touched and in awe. Linda stood beside them, eyes glazed over. Then the three of them hugged, overwhelmed with emotion.

Chapter 15

Linda, Brenda, Emily, and Kelly rode in the car. Linda was still blown away by the new discovery. She asked herself how she could not have seen the signs. Then she thought, easy. Kelly does not have eyes like her sister's, whose witch traits could be seen deep inside her blue eyes. Kelly's eyes appeared black, so it never crossed her mind to think of her as a witch. She knew Emily was one and would someday have to deal with it, but with Kelly she never thought about it. And the witch sense that she felt in the house, other than her own, she assumed was just Emily's.

"That's why she chose me. Wow. I never understood it until now," Linda said, still in disbelief. She turned around looking at Kelly.

"So, my grandmother was a witch?" Kelly asked for the first time, curious about her biological family. She was always so loved by her parents, and never had a need to know much about her biological family. She knew what Linda knew, which was that her mother passed away giving birth and that was it.

"She must have been a witch," Linda replied, tickled. "And I'm sure your biological mother or father, or both, were, too." Her eyes lit up with excitement. "I mean, you do have to be an extremely gifted witch to sense other witches out in the open where there are lots of people. It's a very rare attribute for a witch to possess. Hey, I was living with you and it never crossed my mind, being that I knew Emily was a witch."

Linda shook her head at the thought of it, her eyes welling up, finally at a loss for words. Emily hugged Kelly, ecstatic.

"You're a witch after all. Now I don't have to be a freak all by myself," Emily said with glee. They all laughed.

"Who you calling a freak?" Brenda said playfully.

"Just playing," Emily replied, hands up.

"So that's why you guys like to sleep in the woods, to use the trees as weapons?" Kelly asked.

"That's one reason," Linda answered. "It's also out in the open so we can typically see or hear them coming. And a tree makes a great shield. Also, if we we're killed, we can protect our anonymity. We can't have people seeing us evaporating into ashes in public."

"Talk about creating an all-out witch hunt," Brenda added.

"Look you guys. Speaking of woods, we're not out of them yet. There're still people who want us dead," Linda said, reminding them of the severity of the situation.

"Why do they wanna kill us so bad?" Emily asked.

Linda answered her the same way her mother answered her when she was Emily's age. Carefully.

"They think we're evil because we're different, and they don't understand us. And when people don't understand something or it's different, it makes them uncomfortable and fearful. So they want to destroy it. These kinds of people have been around since the beginning of time," Linda said, looking at her two girls with kind eyes. She wanted them to know that there was nothing wrong with them and that being a witch is something that they could be proud of. "You girls are part of a very small group of people, who have always from the very beginning contributed wonderful things to the world. And most of the world has no idea these people were witches." She sighed; she wanted her girls to heed her words carefully. "You are special. And you're going to do great things in life. So no matter what someone may say to you, don't ever think that being a witch is a curse, because it's not... it's a gift." Her daughters followed her every word. Linda thought about her own words, realizing that she forgot that herself. Her girls smiled.

"So if a person has a gun, does that make them evil or good?" Brenda added. The girls thought about it.

"It depends on who's holding the gun and their intentions," Emily said, proud of her answer.

"Exactly. It's the same thing with witchcraft," Brenda said, schooling the girls.

"So we're just special," Kelly said, looking at Emily with a witty smile.

"Yeah, special," Emily reiterated, amused.

Linda gave a smirk and shook her head, seeing that they were toying with her. She was amused by her daughters' humor, knowing that when her own mother gave her the same talk, she took it much more serious. However, she also knew that her girls understood—and just a couple of weeks ago they were in sunny California living the life of typical teenaged girls.

Linda felt the car speeding up and looked at Brenda.

"What's wrong?"

"The twins are waving me up to the side of their car," Brenda said. She sped up.

"Why don't they just call?" Linda said.

"Because they're special, too," Emily said with a laugh. Kelly laughed as well, while Brenda and Linda shook their heads, not giving in to the laughter that bubbled up inside them.

"The twins don't have phones," Brenda said, pulling alongside them. "Carrie must already be on the phone."

When they pulled beside Carrie, they could see she was indeed on her phone. Rhonda hung her head out of the window, her hair whipping all over her face like a rag doll's.

"We're stopping at the next gas station," Rhonda shouted. She looked like something was wrong.

They all pulled into the gas station. Carrie, the Woody brothers, and the twins got out of their car. Carrie was on her phone. She looked distraught; the twins looked worried. Linda pulled up right behind them and they got out as well. They gathered around Carrie, waiting to hear what was going on.

"Yeah, yeah, okay. Okay. Okay…" She hung up the phone and stared first at her daughters and then Linda, Brenda, the Woody brothers, and the girls.

"What happened?" Linda asked.

"Mom. She's had a heart attack," Carrie said as she swallowed the lump in her throat.

They all were devastated. Tears welled up.

"Is she okay?" Brenda asked.

"Yes, she's okay. But I don't know…" Carrie said.

"What do you mean you don't know?" Linda said.

"They said… she's recovering well. But I got a feeling they're just telling me that because we're in danger."

"I thought you could feel it if she was in pain," Emily said.

"Well, yes, but mom is a very strong woman," Brenda said. "And I don't think she wants to alarm us."

"So we're going back?" Linda asked.

"I could tell the cousins were hiding something, 'cause they knew we'd want to come back," Carrie said, letting the conversation play over in her head.

"So let's go," Brenda said.

"Brenda, it's not that simple. We have kids to consider," Carrie said. The twins and the girls looked at each other.

"Let's go," the twins and girls said in unison. They knew the risk they were taking but none of them cared. Linda looked at her girls unsure, but she wanted to go back as well.

"Heck, we can get killed out here on these roads. Besides, voting booths are all jacked up in Florida anyway and I look forward to voting," Kelly said. They all couldn't help but smile, knowing that this could be very dangerous.

Carrie looked at Linda and Brenda, who seemed eager to go back home. The girls nodded, wanting to go back, too.

"Maybe going back home would be the last thing any of the witch hunters would expect," Emily said. Kelly nodded nervously.

"Not the true witch hunter that sighted us. He's going to know we're going back. It will literally be like going into the lion's den," Carrie said, with a heavy sigh. They all stood waiting for someone to say something.

"Well, I can't wait to go to North Carolina," Zach said, making eye contact with Taylor, both eager for a fight.

"You'll love it," Emily said with a half-smile. "You know, with all the sights to see and stuff."

"Linda?" Carrie asked, looking for confirmation—after all, they had kids to think about. They looked at each other, understanding the danger of the decision.

"Well, that's it. Let's go back home," Linda said.

Chapter 16

As they followed Carrie's SUV down the highway, Linda addressed her kids from the passenger seat.

"Look, they're going to be coming after us, and who knows what kind of independent agents they get to assist them." Linda held her girls' hands, looking very serious. "The head witch hunter who saw us through *obviously* only Thomas's eyes is very powerful and smart. He knows all of our weaknesses. And our strengths. Witch hunters with the power to see through humans are very rare and considered master witch hunters."

Linda sighed, not sure about their decision to return home.

"I want you to stay at a hotel when we get back, until we get this thing sorted out. You guys will be safe there. Now that we know it wasn't Kelly's human eyes that alerted him. So you'll be safe."

"So they saw us through Thomas's eyes?" Kelly asked, worried.

"Yes."

"Has he been in danger this whole time?"

Linda hesitated. "He's not my child. You are. I have to worry about you first."

"Mom!" Kelly said, horrified.

"Kelly. Nothing for any of us is promised but death." Linda knew that witch hunters typically didn't kill people who weren't witches. But there were always exceptions.

Kelly understood her mother. And the words *nothing for any of us is promised but death* echoed in her mind.

Her family was at war and there were already casualties. And although death is tragic, it was understood by their family that death is not an end to life but a transitional phase to it. Life is too great and the universe is too vast to be capsulated in just one form. The body houses our spirit, and when the body no longer can accomplish that function for the spirit, it moves on to the next stage. So although there is pain, when it comes to the passing of a witch, a human, or even a witch hunter, it is not the end.

Kelly remembered how her mother used to talk to her about death, explaining that you can either have a bad death or a beautiful one. And that if you're standing for something, that is a beautiful death. But a bad death is when you have evil intentions, or worse, take your own life because you've given up. No matter how hard or challenging your life is, life is still God's greatest gift and it should be treated as such.

Kelly understood that death eventually comes to us all, like the sun is destined to set, or even a star whose shine fades. She understood the circle of life—now more than ever. And although the pain of losing loved ones still burned like fire, she felt a peace that she had never felt before.

Brenda guided the car down the long road, as Linda slept in the passenger seat. Kelly was asleep in the back seat. Sitting beside her, Emily made a pen levitate, eyes wide with excitement. The pen kept falling in her lap. Brenda looked at Emily in the rearview mirror amused. Emily tried again, giving it more zing; this time the pen spiraled out of control and landed in Kelly's lap. Kelly was still asleep, leaning against her door, hair covering most of her face.

As Emily grabbed the pen, she noticed that Kelly's clothes were wet. She reached for her sister's hand and felt the wetness there, too. When Emily realized that Kelly's shirt was soaked, she pulled her hair back and saw she was sweating profusely.

"Kelly, are you okay?"

Kelly didn't respond.

"Kelly, wake up. Mom, something's wrong with Kelly. She's all wet. Mom!"

Linda sat up and looked back at Emily. Brenda looked in the rearview mirror.

"Something's wrong with Kelly," Emily said.

"What are you talking about?" Linda reached into the back seat, feeling Kelly's cheeks and forehead.

"What?" Kelly slurred.

"Are you okay?" Linda asked.

"I don't know," Kelly said with a moan.

"Kelly?" Linda shook the woozy Kelly's face. "Look at me, sweetie." Linda felt Kelly's forehead again for a temperature. "She's burning up. Kelly, baby, sit up!" Linda said, as she straightened her up.

Brenda reached back and felt her head as best she could while driving.

"Oh, my goodness, she's hot! She has the strain," Brenda said.

"Yeah," Linda concurred.

"What's the strain?" Emily asked. No one answered her, too occupied with Kelly. "What's the strain?!"

"Witches sometimes get the strain when they first come into their powers. They overheat," Brenda said.

"We need to get some ice and cool her off," Linda said.

Kelly moaned and squirmed.

"Just hang in there, baby," Linda said, feeling Kelly's head again. "Her head is like fire."

Brenda reached back to feel as well. "Yeah," she confirmed.

"Mom, is she going to be okay?" Emily started to panic.

"She's going to be fine," Linda said, unsure. She looked at Brenda, who looked as worried as she did. They both had seen people who had the strain after they came into their power. They were hot, too, but nowhere near this hot.

They punched it and passed Carrie's car, waving for them to follow.

They pulled into a mini-mart gas station. Brenda jumped out and rushed into the store. Linda got into the back seat with Kelly.

Carrie, the Woody brothers, and the twins got out of their car.

"What now?" Shonda asked.

"It just doesn't stop," Rhonda added.

"Will you two shut up?" Carrie said. Carrie went over to Brenda's car and saw Kelly looking sick and sweating. When the twins saw it was a serious situation, their smiles quickly vanished. Carrie felt Kelly's head. "Oh my God!" she said. Linda continued to rub the top of Kelly's head, comforting her. Kelly's eyes rolled to the back of her head, as she struggled to stay conscious. Brenda ran back to the car with two bags of ice and dumped them all over Kelly and Linda. Everyone looked at Brenda like she was crazy. She shrugged, apologetic. Linda took the ice and rubbed it all over Kelly's body.

"Linda, if you don't get this fever down..." Brenda said.

"I know, I know!" Linda said, knowing Kelly could die. She looked at Emily reassuringly. "Come on, Kelly. Come on, sweetie. Yeah. We just have to cool her down, that's all. She's going to be fine," Linda said as she continued to rub ice over Kelly's chest and neck while rocking her back and forth.

Emily watched, eyes wide, while rubbing ice on Kelly's legs. This continued for about twenty minutes.

Brenda came back with more ice every few minutes. There were at least fifteen empty ice bags on the ground beside the car, and the whole back seat was soaked because the ice melted so fast on Kelly's hot body.

Kelly trembled and began to pant.

"Mom, she's shaking!" Emily said.

Kelly grimaced in pain, biting down on her bottom lip. They watched her shake.

"Oh my goodness," Brenda said, sympathizing with Kelly, and with Linda as a mother.

"No. This is a good sign," Linda said.

Carrie felt her head again. "Linda, she's still hot," Carrie said.

Linda felt her head once again. "Kelly, baby. Are you feeling better?" she asked, looking into Kelly's eyes.

"Mom. I feel like I'm on fire," Kelly said as tears fell from her eyes. She winced, breathing hard.

"I know, baby. Just focus on your breathing. Slower, slower, slower," Linda said, continuing to rub ice on her.

"Why is this happening?" Kelly asked, her eyes pleading for the pain to stop.

"It just does to some witches," Linda replied.

"You?" Kelly asked.

"No. My mother. She had it," Linda said.

"And Uncle Waterson," Brenda said.

"Just slow your breathing down... That's it," Linda coached as she placed her hand on Kelly's chest, using her hand as a guide. Everyone watched intently as Kelly started to look better, and her breathing eased. After feeling her daughter's forehead, a smile crept across Linda's face. When Kelly saw her mother smiling, she knew she was going to be okay. Everyone else smiled as well, relieved that Kelly would be fine.

"Good," Carrie said.

"That was a little scary," Brenda said.

"Yeah, 'cause witches sometimes die from that," Taylor said matter-of-factly. Everyone looked at Taylor with a bit of disdain and disbelief.

"Will you shut up?!" Zach exclaimed. Taylor gave an apologetic shrug. "What, it's true," he said under his breath.

Kelly looked up at the Woody brothers and smiled.

Linda and Kelly looked at each other and sighed. Emily kissed Kelly on the forehead.

"Let's get on the road. You guys make sure you have your cells on," Carrie said.

"Okay," Linda replied.

They all looked at each other with smiles and relief. Emily and Brenda used a bunch of tiles to soak up the water in the back seat and floor that was left by the melted ice. Then the family gassed up their vehicles and hit the road.

As Linda drove, she kept an eye on Kelly. They drove for hours. Linda took in the beautiful landscape on the side of the road. The sunset sat on the hillside perfectly, cascading a luminous light off the vast hills and grass. Linda's tired eyes smiled at the beauty and calmness of it all.

Brenda looked back at Emily as she twirled a pen in the air, frustrated because it kept falling. She then looked at Kelly, who was twirling a bunch of pencils and quarters, nickels, dimes, and pennies as if she was conducting a symphony. Emily struggled with her pen, distracted and peeved by Kelly's extravaganza.

"When you move things, you have to learn how to breathe," Brenda said. The girls both let out deep breaths. "From your gut," Brenda said, showing them how. Their objects spun faster, with Emily's still falling in her lap every few seconds.

"Girls, you have to also remember that to be a witch comes with responsibility. You can never, ever abuse your power in any way," Linda said.

"Even though it is pretty cool," Brenda said. Linda and Brenda smiled.

"Witches consider there to be three places of consciousness. Being in the moment. Being conscious of the moment. And being completely out of body. A very difficult place to get to," Linda explained, talking with her hands. "These places of consciousness help center a witch's power. They also help you to stay in control."

"Do you think being in the moment is the best place to be?" Kelly asked.

"Smart," Brenda said to Linda, amused.

"It is. That's where your core power lies," Linda replied.

"Well…" Brenda looked at Emily frustrated and amused, as she struggled with her gravitating pen. "For most of us."

"Why you looking at me?" Emily said. They all laughed. "I'm getting it," Emily said, focused on her spinning pen.

Linda continued to drive through the night, following Carrie's SUV.

Chapter 17

G imon and the rest of the witch hunters sat under the stars around a campfire in the woods. Gimon schooled some of the younger witch hunters on what was to come, reading passages from a book his grandfather gave to his father and his father gave to him. The book was a *Witch Hunters Guide*. It broke down the principles and the different stages of being a witch hunter. He wanted them to know what they were doing was God's work and was biblical. And the apocalypse was near.

The young witch hunters stared at Gimon in admiration. He read them passages under the stars so they could see how they were all connected to the stars and ultimately the universe. He clutched the tattered leatherbound book and continued to explain the importance of their work.

"I want you guys to know what we are doing is dangerous work, and when we come across this family we can't show them any mercy. They have to be terminated with extreme prejudice." His eyes showed the seriousness of what he was saying, as he looked at the witch hunters around the campfire. "Life has to have order. People need order. We are the people that keep that order... I don't like killing witches. Especially young witches. Part of me hates it. But I will shoot a baby right in the heart... if it's a witch. Because baby witches grow up to be adult witches, and they are an abomination to our world. These witches who are not human and harness power are dangerous. And

Christopher J. Moore

they will kill you if they get the chance. I saw my mother
die at the hands of a coven when I was seven. My mother
hid me in the attic, and she tried to convince them she was
not a witch hunter. She said her husband was one, but she
was not. And she wasn't. But they killed her anyway."
Gimon let his words sink in, still feeling the sting of his
mother's loss. "We are the protectors of our world. Where
witches with the trait hide among human witches in plain
sight. Understand, human witches have power, too; it's just
a different type of power. Their power lies more in prayer,
not telekinetic power. So we don't hunt those kind of
witches. But the family we are hunting does possess a
telekinetic power, going back five generations at least. I felt
it. That means they can knock you off of your feet and
break your neck like a twig."

Gimon stared at the campfire, the flames reflecting in
his eyes. The others sat there watching him, hanging on his
every word. Silence filled the campsite, broken only by the
elements of nature and the crackling of burning wood.
Gimon snapped out of his trance, looking at all of the eyes
on him. He sighed.

"First time I ever killed a witch. I was only nine. I
went out with my grandpa and my uncle to track down a
coven of witches that my grandfather said were hiding in
the swamps. My dad was out of town that week on
business. He was a truck driver. Well let's just say my
grandfather used my father being out of town as an
opportunity to take me out and do some hunting. I think
nine is too young for any boy to kill anything. But my
grandfather thought you could never be too young. So
when I shot one of them for the first time and saw their
bodies turn into ash, and evaporate into thin air right before
my very eyes, I knew that I wasn't killing a person. But a

141

thing. A thing that's not human. A thing that's evil and will do evil things. A thing that's out of line with nature. It was at that moment that I knew we were not murderers. But merchants of justice. People who make things right in the world that's wrong. I know my father would not have wanted his young son out there killing witches. But thank God for my grandfather... who showed me what they really are. Ashes... walking around like humans. And the fact that they turn into ashes and evaporate into thin air gives us the power to kill witches without having to deal with the law, because there's just no evidence," he said with a mischievous laugh.

The other witch hunters laughed as well until Gimon suddenly stopped laughing. His eyes slowly rolled back in his head and then his eyes closed shut. The witch hunters stopped laughing and looked at each other, perplexed. Then Gimon's eyes slowly opened. He felt a very familiar sting in his chest, knowing their prey was near. His eyes narrowed and a sour expression came over him. Then he smiled, as if he took a bite of his favorite food. The other witch hunters mimicked his smile with their own inane ones.

"No time for rest tonight. Tonight we drive," Gimon said. Smiles once again disappeared.

Chapter 18

L inda continued to drive into the night.
Thomas had not answered his phone since the
incident.

Kelly and Emily slept, leaning on each other in the
back seat.

Brenda was dozing off as well. She shook her head
and looked at Linda. Linda looked more tired than her.
"Are you okay?" she asked.

"Yeah, I'm fine," Linda replied.

"Well, let me know if you need me to drive."

"I need you to drive," Linda replied with a smile.
They laughed.

Linda pulled to the side of the road. Linda and Brenda
got out of the car and switched sides.

Brenda put on her seatbelt, but her attention went to
a car that slowed down as it passed going the other way. She
noticed there were reflectors all around the car. Her heart
sank. She quickly shifted the gear and sped off.

"What's wrong?" Linda asked.

"It's them," Brenda answered.

Linda quickly turned around. She saw nothing. "You
sure?"

"They had reflectors all around their car," Brenda
said.

Linda looked back. Her eyes widened at the sight of
headlights coming up fast from behind. She looked at how

fast Brenda was driving and then at the headlights rapidly approaching.

"They're coming... fast," Linda said as she saw the car in hot pursuit.

As they sped down the road, Linda watched the car gaining on them. She hoped this was just their paranoia and that the car would get off on the next exit. Or maybe it was a husband trying to get his pregnant wife to the hospital before she had the baby in the back seat. But she knew better. She nudged the girls.

"Emily, Kelly, wake up. We're going to get hit by some witch hunters. So brace yourself," she said in a calm voice.

The girls turned around as the car closed in on them. Their eyes went wide, full of fear.

"Stop them, mom!" Emily exclaimed.

"I can't. They have reflectors," Linda said.

"So," Kelly said, heart beating twice as fast.

"The shock wave can bounce back on to us," Linda explained. "It's an old witch hunter trick but very effective."

"Oh my God!" Emily said, as they braced for impact. The car flashed its high beams and smashed into them. The girls screamed. The car swerved, almost losing control and running off into a deep ditch.

Brenda looked at the ditch they almost perished in. She checked the rearview mirror, watching the car behind them. She had the pedal hard to the floor. Linda looked at the ditch on her side minimizing as they drove.

"Mom, they're going to kill us!" Kelly said.

"Mom!" Emily said.

"Go, Brenda!" Linda yelled.

Brenda drove as fast as she could. She saw a car up ahead and swerved past it. The car with reflectors swerved to avoid the car as well. The pursuing car flashed its high beams once again and slammed into them a second time. Both of the cars spun violently. Brenda pumped the brakes, hoping that luck was on their side. Her car stopped in the middle of the road, sending up a cloud of smoke all around. The car behind them went off into a shallow ditch.

Brenda, Linda and the girls sighed hard, relieved. They stared through the thick smoke at the car in the ditch. Linda and Brenda looked at each other, surprised the car wasn't in worse shape. They assumed the ditch was deeper, than it was. Their eyes widened as the car with reflectors lit up and backed out of the ditch. A passing car pulled over to see if everyone was okay. Unfortunately for the Switch family, the car with the reflectors was okay as well. Brenda looked at Linda and punched it again.

Brenda kept her eyes on the road while Linda and the girls all turned around, watching. There was no sign of the car pursuing them. Then the familiar headlights came into view.

"Faster, faster, faster!" Linda exclaimed.

"I'm trying!" Brenda applied as much pressure to the gas pedal as possible, trying to get maximum speed out of their car.

The car approached from behind preparing for another hit to the bumper. Linda extended her hand toward the back window and sent a purple blast that bounced off the car's reflectors making the rear of their car slide to the right, and almost flip over. They screamed. Brenda got the car back under control, then looked at Linda as if she was crazy. Linda shrugged with an *oops* expression.

"Please don't do that again," Brenda said.

"Thought I'd give it a shot," Linda said.

Brenda drove as fast as she could, the other car right behind them.

"Hey, there's Carrie!" Brenda said, catching sight of Carrie up ahead.

When they finally caught up to Carrie, Brenda pulled up on the side of her.

Carrie could see the car trailing her. She also noticed the reflectors. The twins sat in the back seat staring at the car, noticing the reflectors, too. The Woody brothers looked at each other ready to send out a purple blast, but the twins stopped them.

"They have reflectors," the twins said.

"All right," they said, desperately wanting to engage.

Carrie pointed to the exit up ahead. She punched the gas pedal and led the way, with Brenda right behind her, and the car with reflectors close behind them. Brenda realized that the pursuing car was purposely laying back.

"I wonder why they're slowing down." Brenda said. Linda watched the car, baffled as well. They sped off the exit and got the answer; three Jeeps and a Hummer were waiting, with their headlights off. As Carrie and Brenda got closer, their lights turned on, all armed with reflectors.

"Oh my goodness," Linda said. Kelly and Emily sat in the back seat, terrified. Carrie crashed into one of the Jeeps, clearing a path for Brenda. Carrie and Brenda drove as fast as they could, while the witch hunters pursued them. One of the three Jeeps rammed Carrie's car. Another one did the same to Linda's.

"Turn here," Linda said. Brenda made a hard right turn, avoiding one of the Jeeps. The Hummer was right on her bumper. Linda turned around and could see the shadowy figures in the Hummer. They sped up to the side of Linda's car. They all looked straight into the eyes of Gimon. He gave a satisfied smile, and looked rather calm for someone who was in a high-speed chase. Brenda shot in front of Carrie's car. Both of them driving as fast as possible.

Brenda sped off the road and headed for the woods, with Carrie right behind her. They rode through a large field hitting dips every ten yards. The Jeeps were definitely at an advantage, handling the off road much better. As they all sped toward the woods, Linda and Carrie's cars bounced up and down, bashing their front bumpers into pieces.

They drove by a parked trailer and then a farmhouse. Linda took off her seatbelt as they got closer to the tree line bordering the woods.

"Take off your seatbelts you guys," Linda said.

"We're almost there," Brenda said, determined to get them to the woods.

They all unbuckled their seatbelts.

"When we stop, you guys run as fast as you can into the woods. Don't look back, just run," Linda said, staring deep into her girls' eyes so they understood the importance of doing exactly what she said.

"You're not coming?" Kelly asked.

"No, we need to give you guys a head start," Linda said. The girls nodded in agreement. "But we'll catch up," Linda added.

Brenda shot between two trees, knocking off Linda's right side view mirror. Carrie followed, cutting through the brush.

"Ready... go!" Brenda said as she came to a sliding halt, sending a cloud of dirt into the air.

"Run! Run, you guys!" Linda shouted.

Doors flew open on both cars. Brenda and Linda hopped out. They stirred the dirt in the air, sending a tornado to the witch hunter's trucks. The witch hunters stayed in their trucks firing their guns out of their windows.

Kelly and Emily bolted through the woods. They wanted to go back to help but knew their skills and powers were too weak, and so they would do more harm than good.

Carrie, the Woody brothers, and the twins took cover behind their car. Brenda and Linda did the same. Bullets rained down on both cars. The twins first showed fear, then strength in their eyes, staring at each other as they remained behind their car. Zach and Taylor had a look of excitement. They were trained and prepared, and extremely eager to fight. They looked at each other and shared a nervous laugh, waiting for the gunfire to stop.

When it finally stopped, silence filled the woods. Both sides were waiting for someone to make the next move.

Chapter 19

T he witch hunters' doors flew open and they came out shooting. Each one held a reflector shield in one hand while shooting with the other.

Linda, her sisters, the Woody brothers, and the twins shot shock waves at the witch hunters. Some of the witch hunters' reflectors bounced the shock waves off; some witch hunters were thrown into trees. The other witch hunters took cover behind trees and continued to fire their automatic weapons. The Woody brothers sent out a blast, knocking a witch hunter into the air and into a tree branch. They gave each other a high five, then ran from a hail of bullets, jumping and flipping their way to safety. They realized there was no time for celebrating. Switch family members looked at the Woody Brothers, impressed with their power and agility.

Kelly and Emily ran, hearing gun fire exploding like fireworks. Then it abruptly ended. The girls stopped, horrified, then turned around. They couldn't see anything but the blackness of the wilderness. They looked at each other, thinking the same thing. Did the gunfire stop because their mother and newfound family prevailed, or because they were dead?

"Should we go back?" Kelly asked, her heart racing. Emily stared at her, eyes vacant with fear.

"Emily!" Kelly said, making her snap out of it.

"I don't know. Mom said to just keep running," Emily said, looking around. "Maybe we should just do that. After all, this whole thing is like déjà vu."

"You right about that. We seem to be always running in the woods... Think they made it?" Kelly said, emotional and overwhelmed.

"I don't know..." Emily answered, unsure of anything. Her eyes narrowed, focused on something deep in the woods. She could only see tree branches moving toward them at top speed. Her face morphed to fear. Kelly looked at what Emily was looking at, and her fear showed as well. They watched, eyes wide.

Suddenly, Linda, Carrie, Brenda, the Woody brothers, and the twins emerged from the darkness, running full speed.

"Girls, run!" Linda screamed. Kelly and Emily turned back around and ran as fast as they could.

Gimon led his men after the Switch family, directing them to spread out.

The Switch family slid down hills and ran through a small creak. Eventually they lost the witch hunters and stopped running. They caught their breath and looked around before they continued to trek through the woods.

"Where are we going?" Kelly asked.

"I don't know," Linda said.

"This is crazy," Emily said.

"Should we spread out?" Linda said to Carrie.

"No. Let's stay together," Carrie replied.

As they trudged through the woods, they looked for anything that could help them. Linda looked up at the stars, hoping they would guide them back to the road.

"Are we really out here in the woods running for our lives?" Kelly said to Emily, slightly amused at the ridiculousness of their circumstances. "I keep thinking I'm going to wake up any moment back in San Diego."

"Me, too," Emily said. "Shonda, has this ever happened to you guys before?"

"No. Well, once some guy was following me and Rhonda and my mom around the mall. It kind of freaked us out, but that's pretty much the extent of it."

Carrie chimed in, "There are a lot of people who are wanna be witch hunters, and try to look for witches. They're amateurs, so they're really not that much of a threat. They have a whole network of people out there sharing information on the Internet, all trying to track witches—who they consider not to be human. But unless they have the gift of *sight*, they usually come up with nothing. And whoever they're pursuing, they never know for sure if they possess our unique power. Imagine if a witch hunter shot a witch who didn't turn into ashes and evaporate into thin air. There would be a crime scene and they'd be on the hook for murder. Now for the hunt to be real there must be at least one witch hunter with the gift of sight."

"Sight?" Kelly said, not sure what Carrie meant.

"Like the witch hunters who saw our ritual, through your... well Thomas's eyes," Linda said to Kelly, "and then your grandmother could see through theirs. That's her special gift."

"Do we all have special gifts?" Emily asked.

"Of course. Just like regular people have special gifts," Brenda added.

"And these people chasing us, one of them obviously has the gift of sight?" Kelly asked.

"Yes," Carrie said. "They're the real thing."

"How do you know?" Emily asked.

"You can feel a master witch hunter," Linda said.

Carrie added to her sister's comment. "The older you get the more you can feel. A witch hunter always tracks through the eldest witch's eyes on *sight*. That's why your grandmother felt him first. Then he's able to continue to track the witches who have the closest bond with the elder witch. Which is why some family members could go back home. The witch hunter coming after us knows what he's doing. You kill the witches closest to the elder and the elder breaks down. Making it so they're mentally unstable and easier to be captured and killed," Carrie said.

"This is all too much, for even me," Rhonda said. They looked at her and laughed as they continued to stomp through the woods.

"I'm sick of running. I say we go back and fight," Brenda said.

"I think that's a terrible idea," Linda said.

"Here, here," Carrie added. "Let's just keep walking until we hit a road. We should be hitting one soon."

"I'm tired," Shonda said.

"Why can't we just call the police?" Emily asked her mom.

"Because if they see some of us turned to ashes, we would be forever pursued and studied like lab rats for the rest of our lives, and our secret will be out forever," Linda said.

"Well, who wants to be a lab rat? I think I'd rather die fighting," Kelly said.

"Who knows, you just might get your wish," Shonda said.

Kelly and Emily looked at Shonda.

"I was just playing," Shonda said, realizing she was being a jerk.

"No, she wasn't," Rhonda added. "That's just her." The girls and the twins all looked at each other and laughed.

They heard a branch snap. They froze, staring in the direction of the crackling brush.

"Run!" Brenda screamed. They all bolted. Gimon ran after them, the rest of the witch hunters behind him.

"Finally," Gimon said, a crazed glint in his eyes.

"Is this the family?" one of the witch hunters asked, feeling the excitement in the air. They continued to run hard.

"Yes!" Gimon replied.

They chased them until Gimon ordered them to stop and wait for his orders. They didn't see the witches but they knew they were out there, trying to be as quiet as possible. Gimon reached into his bag and pulled out a pair of night vision goggles. He could see a couple of them moving very slowly, trying not to be seen or heard.

"Here we go," Gimon said, watching the Woody brothers.

"What do you want us to do?" Mason asked.

"Let the others go first. They brought us in the woods for a reason." Mason signaled the other witch hunters to run after them. "Go get 'em!" he shouted.

"This is going to be fun," Gimon said with glee.

"Yeah," Cam said.

The witch hunters charged the Switch family, firing their guns, making them come out to fight. Linda fired off a shock wave, knocking one of them into a tree and breaking his back.

Brenda sent a shock wave at another witch hunter, who blocked it with his reflector. The Switch family fought with all of their skills—except for Emily and Kelly, who took cover, staying out of sight. They were surrounded and were being closed in on.

Gimon watched as the witch hunters and the Switch family and Woody brothers battled in the open field. He smiled as if he was watching a chess match where the master chess player was defeated before he knew it. He then saw Kelly and Emily hiding behind a huge tree.

Linda and Carrie were back to back, sending powerful shock waves at the witch hunters. The fighting continued, with gunfire and purple lighting up the sky.

Gimon crept up behind Emily and Kelly and grabbed them both.

"Enough!" Gimon shouted.

When the Switch family saw Gimon had the girls, they stopped cold. Linda put her hands down, heartbroken—she had no more fight left in her. Taylor was about to send a blast at Gimon, but Zach stopped him.

The witch hunters tied them all up against three trees. They packed wood around their feet ready to set them on fire. Gimon and his cronies approached the tied-up family, reveling in what was about to happen.

"This is a great day for me. And, unfortunately, a bad one for you," Gimon said.

"Yeah. Bad for you," Cam said.

"What do you want?" Carrie asked.

"Come on now. You know what I want. I want your ashes to fly to the heavens. Or should I say to hell," Gimon said with a smug grin.

"Why don't you just shoot us then? What are you waiting for?" Brenda shouted.

"Well, this is kind of nostalgia for me. I want your ashes to go up the old-fashioned way," Gimon said as he grabbed Brenda by the chin.

"You are such a coward and a waste of a life," Linda said, fuming with anger.

"A waste of a life? Killing witches is my life." Gimon got in Linda's face, staring deep in her eyes, seeing the witch inside her. Linda's blue eyes possessed electric currents deep within.

"You're despicable," Linda said with disdain, then spat in his face. He smiled, as if this moment was not going to be ruined for any reason, especially a little spit. He wiped the spit off his face, still beaming with pride, looking at all of the witches tied up. He stared into Carrie's eyes.

"I can see the witch in all of your eyes. Your souls are already dead," Gimon said.

"No. Your soul is dead," Linda shot back.

"My soul?" Gimon said. All of the witch hunters laughed.

"You can at least let the girls go," Linda said. Gimon smiled. He walked over to Emily and Kelly. He looked into Emily's blue eyes. He smiled. Then he looked at Kelly.

"Sweetheart, how did you ever get caught up with such a sort?" he asked Kelly, touching her cheek, staring into her dark brown eyes.

"They're my family," Kelly said.

Gimon looked over at his men and they all laughed. "They're not your family, sweetheart. Just some people you've been living with, obviously," Gimon said with a devilish grin. "Let this one go."

"You sure?" Mason asked.

"Yeah, who she gonna tell? There won't be anything left but ashes anyway." Stem untied Kelly. Kelly looked at her mother who mouthed... *go.*

"Mom," Kelly stammered, horrified by what was going to happen to her family. Linda just nodded. Then two witch hunters led her away. Kelly reached out for her sister, but the witch hunters pulled her away. "Mom!" Kelly cried out.

The witch hunters led Kelly away through the woods.

Chapter 20

G imon stood in front of the witch hunters as they stacked more wood around the tied-up Switch family and Woody brothers. Linda looked at Emily with loving eyes as tears rolled down her daughter's scared face. The twins looked more angry than scared. And the Woody brothers looked stoic, as if the game was over. Carrie shook her head and looked at her daughters, more scared for them than for herself. Brenda looked at Linda, who showed no more fight in her eyes.

"Should I light them on fire now?" Mason asked.

"No, not yet. I want to enjoy this for a moment," Gimon said, breathing in the fresh air and surveying his surroundings.

Kelly cried as the two witch hunters led her through the woods. She looked at the men leading her away from her family forever, and felt powerless to do anything about it. She tried to concentrate, wanting to use her powers to do something to stop them. But only leaves on the ground swirled by their feet. The witch hunters pulled her along, unaware of the swirling leaves.

Kelly's emotions were all over the place as her frustration grew. She staggered through the woods head hung low, feeling the nadir of her suffering from her head to her toes. Her feet started to drag and she sobbed uncontrollably. One of the witch hunters snatched her up and gave her a hard smack across the cheek. Kelly snapped out of her hysteria, eyes wild from the blow. He let her go and gave a cold stare, then he grabbed her hard by the arm and continued to lead her away.

With a witch hunter on each arm, Kelly noticed the leaves falling from the branches high up in the trees, as if something was shaking them off. The witch hunters soon noticed this as well.

Kelly started to shake as tears continued to fall from her eyes. Her pupils started to dilate and her hands began to heat up. She looked down at them, feeling what seemed like fire.

The two witch hunters holding her felt the heat. They looked at each other, then at Kelly.

Her pupils continued to dilate and her heart beat faster and faster—it felt like a drum roll. Her hands glowed red. She looked down at them, scared. Her eyes closed. The adrenalin in her body rose like a phoenix. Her eyes fluttered, then opened. She knew that things were different—she was out of her body and driven by pure instinct.

She looked at the witch hunters, then blasted them in opposite directions, hurling them into trees. If that didn't kill them, surely it left them unable to ever walk again.

Kelly stared at her hands, feeling the power she possessed. She turned in the direction from whence she came... and took off. She ran as fast as she could, jumping over a huge ditch effortlessly. Her eyes were sharply focused as she ran faster with each step.

Linda, Emily, Brenda, Carrie, the Woody brothers, and the twins stood waiting to be burned alive. Stem poured gasoline from an old can at their feet. Gimon, Mason, and Cam all lit torches.

"You people are an abomination. Sent here from the depths of hell. You are a menace to all that is righteous in the world," Gimon said.

"What has any witch ever done to you?" Linda asked with pleading eyes, looking at Emily's tears.

Gimon didn't respond, but his eyes showed that her question had an effect on him. And not a good one.

"Linda, don't waste your breath," Carrie said.

"Just let the girls go!" Linda cried out.

"Now you know I can't do that," Gimon said, showing no mercy in his expression.

The witch hunters raised their torches, ready to light the funeral pyre. They waited on Gimon, giving him the satisfaction of being the first one to set the witches on fire. The members of the Switch family gave each other a final look, as did the Woody brothers.

Gimon placed his torch next to the gasoline-drenched wood, but paused for a split second at Linda's sudden change of expression.

Linda's eyes went wide when she saw Kelly running out of the woods, coming straight for them. Gimon turned and saw her approaching. Linda's heart sank, wanting her daughter to stay out of harm's way. However, she noticed the red hands Kelly now possessed as she ran toward them, enraged. Kelly pointed the palms of her hands at them. The witch hunters were caught off guard. Then a gust of wind blew out their torches.

"What the?" Gimon said, stunned.

Before they knew what hit them, Kelly blasted two witch hunters at the same time, knocking them into trees. Then she took out several other witch hunters with her red blasts. Two witch hunters went for her, but she blasted them into each other.

Gimon snapped out of his daze and ran for cover deeper in the woods, along with the rest of his crew.

Kelly went after them. She sent a powerful shock wave, creating a huge dirt cloud, knocking all of them off their feet. She closed in, ready to finish them off, feeling the incredible surge of power from within.

"Kelly, no!" Linda screamed, knowing how easily a trap could be waiting for her. Kelly turned around, huffing and puffing, ready for war. She looked delirious as she slowly calmed down, her eyes still wild. She hurried over to her family and quickly untied them. Linda hugged Kelly tightly. They held each other for a moment. The rest of the family stared at her amazed.

"Dang, girl, what was that?" Shonda said.

"That was my sister, that's what that was," Emily said, proud.

"That was so wicked," Rhonda said.

"You know they're not going to stop," Carrie said.

"I know," Linda replied.

"Mom, my hands are burning," Kelly said.

"They'll cool down in a few minutes. Just slow your breathing down, sweetie," Linda said. Kelly took two deep breaths, slowing her breathing.

"Did you know you could do that?" Emily asked.

"Ah, no," Kelly replied, sarcastic. Kelly and Emily shared a smile.

"Well, I'm glad you could," Brenda said, with a big sigh.

"Thank you, baby, for coming back for us," Carrie said, proud and in awe. Carrie and Kelly hugged.

"Of course I was coming back. You're my family," Kelly said. The ladies all hugged, relieved. Even the Woody brothers were hugging people, happy to still be alive, until they looked at each other. Then quickly snapped back into the tough cool guys they were.

"Let's get back to the cars," Linda said, wanting to get her girls completely out of danger.

They hoped the witch hunters' vehicles were still there, which meant they were either dead or too broke up physically to cause any problems for a while.

Sure enough, the witch hunters' trucks and cars were still there. Kelly's blast would have been really difficult to survive; if they did survive it, they would definitely realize that it was in their best interest to stop their pursuits and leave the witches alone until they could regroup. The witch hunters knew that the Switch family would be moving from their old home and that they would no longer have a beacon on them. So for now the family was safe.

And Gimon and his witch hunters would have to live to fight another day. Or at least find a new coven to hunt.

Chapter 21

K elly and Emily rode in the back seat quietly while Linda drove. Brenda stared out of the window in deep thought. They were all exhausted.

Linda could see that Kelly was overwhelmed by what just happened. She had been there herself before, and she remembered what it was like when she first used her powers against someone. Although nowhere near as dramatic as what Kelly had done, it did have an immense effect on her—it prompted her to leave home and run off with the man who became her husband. Even in self-defense, it still takes a piece of your soul when you have to hurt or even kill someone. So she understood what Kelly was dealing with.

"Sweetie, are you okay?" Linda asked, eyes in the rearview mirror.

"Who, me?" Kelly replied, somber.

"Yeah," Linda said.

"I'm fine."

Linda looked at Emily. "Emily?"

"I'm fine, mom."

"This isn't quite the summer vacation I'd hoped for," Linda said, trying to break the tension.

"You telling me," Kelly said with a smirk.

When they finally pulled up in front of the Switch house, across the street they saw a charred skeleton of what used to be Thomas's house. Kelly got out of the car and stared at the rubble. Emily saw Kelly getting emotional.

"Kelly," Emily said, putting a hand on her shoulder. Kelly didn't answer. "Kelly," she repeated.

"Yeah," Kelly replied, despondent.

"Come on," Emily said, turning around.

Carrie, Linda, Brenda, the Woody brothers, and the twins headed up the front porch. The front door opened. They froze.

When Kelly finally turned around, she was stunned by the sight of Dorothy, who was standing on the front porch. Everyone smiled. Suddenly Thomas stepped out from behind Dorothy. Kelly's eyes went wide.

The Switch family watched the two of them, wearing smiles. Taylor looked at his brother as if he missed an opportunity.

"You snooze you lose, bro," Zach said with a smirk and a punch to the arm. Taylor shrugged him off.

Kelly grabbed Thomas by the hand and they strolled through the neighborhood.

"How you feel?" Thomas asked.

"Better. Much better. I thought you were dead," Kelly said.

"I would have called you but my phone was destroyed, along with your number," Thomas said as he kissed the hand he held. "So I couldn't even call you. The price of using your name to call and not knowing your number."

"My mom dropped me off at a party one time, and it was the wrong place and I had forgot my phone. I was stuck. I went to a pay phone and I couldn't call anyone because I didn't know anyone's number. No one's. Not even my mom's number; it just says *mom* on my phone."

They laughed.

"Yeah, it might not hurt to remember a couple of numbers," Thomas said, amused. "Your grandmother seems better."

"Yeah, she's a strong woman. So what exactly happened when we were on the phone?" Kelly asked.

Thomas looked at her and let out a big sigh.

Thomas sat on his couch talking on the phone to Kelly. He noticed two black SUVs pull up in front of the Switch home. Men dressed in all black got out, and they knocked on the front door. Thomas got up and looked through the living room window, still holding the phone with Kelly on the other end. No one answered the door, so the men looked around as they headed back to their trucks, one of the drivers saw Thomas staring at them. Thomas quickly closed the curtains, then slowly peeked from behind them, trying his best not to be seen.

The man by the truck continued to stare at Thomas's house. He signaled the other men and they marched across the street. Thomas peered out through a side curtain, eyes getting wider and wider.

The men walked up to his front door and knocked. Thomas stood against the wall, frozen. They continued to knock until three hard kicks sent the front door off of its hinges. Thomas ran through the house and up the stairs. He dropped his phone and it fell down the stairs and broke apart. One of the men caught him at the top of the stairs and dragged him back down. Thomas punched the man in the jaw and they fought wildly. Then another man grabbed Thomas from behind, and a third man gave a couple blows to Thomas's stomach. Thomas doubled over in pain, trying to catch his breath. One of the men grabbed him by the collar and slammed him up against the wall, questioning him. Thomas shook his head. Another man squirted lighter fluid on the walls and flicked matches, sending the wall up in flames. The man holding Thomas by the collar cocked his fist to punch Thomas again, while drilling him for answers about the Switch family. Thomas shook his head, not saying a word.

Suddenly, Dorothy walked in. She wore a robe and had curlers in her hair. She also had a bag of potato chips in her hand. The men stared at her, dumbfounded. Dorothy put the bag on the nightstand beside her. She smiled, then sent a shock wave, hurling the three men up against the burning wall. She raised an eyebrow, then sent them flying out of the front window and onto the front lawn. Two of their jackets were on fire. She then pointed her hand to the front lawn and the sprinklers came on, putting the fire out. She then took Thomas by the hand and calmly led him outside.

The neighbors watched the spectacle of the three men being arrested while fire fighters fought the blaze. Dorothy gave a police report explaining that she had no idea why those men did what they did. Thomas agreed with Dorothy that the men were mentally unstable, busted down the door, set the house on fire, and jumped out of the front window.

Thomas watched as his house burned, then looked at the men who did it. As they were being taken to jail, they were yelling, *"She's a witch! A real witch!"*

Kelly and Thomas continued to stroll up the street, fingers interlocked.

"Everyone just looked at them like they were crazy. Anyway, she said you guys were okay and you were coming back. I guess she just gets visions sometimes, right?" Thomas asked.

"Yeah, she's unique that way," Kelly said, then had a thought. "Oh man, what did your dad say?" Kelly asked, thinking about their home.

"Thank God we have insurance!"

"Ah, yeah," Kelly replied, relieved. They smiled.

"I have a secret to tell you," Kelly said, wearing a nervous smile.

"What?" Thomas asked.

She thought for a moment, not sure whether to continue. "I just hope you don't look at me too differently."

"What is it?"

Kelly smiled, embarrassed, continuing to have second thoughts.

"What?"

She shook her head as if, *what the heck.*

"You see that trash can?" Kelly asked matter-of-factly.

"Yeah."

She stretched out her hand, closed her eyes for a second, and sent a red shock wave blasting the trash can down the street.

"What the..." Thomas looked at the trash can and then back at Kelly, stunned.

Kelly looked at Thomas, not sure how he took it.

"I found out that my biological mother or father, or both, were witches as well. And my grandmother, too. I guess that's why she picked my mom to raise me."

"Man," he said in awe, trying to process everything.

"Crazy, right?" She shrugged.

Thomas stood there still trying to wrap his brain around it. "Did your mom know?"

"That I was a witch?"

"Yeah."

"No. She had no idea."

"Wow."

"Wow is right," Kelly said, still not being able to grasp this new turn in her life.

Thomas sensed her uneasiness. "Are you okay?" he asked.

Kelly smiled, seeing he was taking it better than she thought he might. And he seemed to be more interested in how she was feeling, than what he thought of her.

"I'm fine. How do you feel about all this?" she asked, giving him a final chance to say *this is way too much for me* and leave her standing alone out there on the street.

Thomas stared at her for a moment. "I don't know. Let me see something." He pulled her to him. He kissed her. She smiled.

"What are you thinking?" she asked.

"Well, your lips still feel the same. so I'm thinking it's okay," he said with a grin.

They kissed again. This time a lot longer. When their lips finally parted, they stared into each other's eyes, feeling the sweet electricity between them.

Thomas's eyes focused down the hill, at the Switch house. "What the heck?"

"What?" Kelly said, still staring lovingly into his eyes. She slowly turned around. "Oh my God!"

Purple flashes came from the Switch house. Kelly's eyes were wide with horror, knowing that something was terribly wrong. She looked at Thomas, and they bolted down the hill. Purple flashes continued to come from the house.

When Kelly got close to the house, she could see the front door was wide open. "Thomas, stay back!"

"No…"

"Thomas, please! Trust me!"

Thomas slowed up, staying behind. Kelly leapt up the front porch and ran inside. To her surprise no one was there. The place was trashed. She looked around, not knowing what to do. Suddenly, the sound of heavy footsteps echoed from the stairway.

It was Gimon. They stared at each other intensely. Kelly was scared but tried not to show it. The much bigger man strolled down the stairs with ease as if he was at home.

"Where is my family?" Kelly asked, giving her best attempt to show strength. He looked at her as if he was a teacher talking to a student after class.

"Who are you?" Gimon said as he continued down the stairs, head cocked.

"Where's my family?" Kelly demanded once again, trying her best to not show she was daunted by his gaze.

He smiled, reading her like an open book. "What I thought I wanted, I realized I don't necessarily need anymore. Because something much more rare has evolved from all of this. I never seen a red witch with my own eyes before. I heard of them. But I thought it was just some old folk tale that came out of the hundreds of stories that people made up as time went by, sitting around campfires. But I know now. It's true. And all that I need now… is you." He gave a smile, looking her up and down like a delicious specimen.

"I want my family."

He stared back at her, fascinated. "Every now and then, God throws you a bone. Something that you didn't quite expect. I once had dreams of leading a normal life. A family with a white picket fence. But this is my life."

"My family?" she said, growing more impatient.

"You…" Gimon said, as he rubbed his hands together slowly. His eyes full of excitement.

Kelly's anger grew as she stood there feeling like he was stalling and her family was somewhere being hurt or even killed.

"You're a special witch, I felt it. There're only six master families in the world that are witches. They all represent their own color. But now I've learned that's not true. Yours makes seven. And your color I'm sure you already know is red. Now to kill a red witch, if the legend is true, can make you one of the most powerful witch hunters to ever walk the earth. Red witches are so rare. Most people don't even try to seek them. But I figured that just maybe you might make it easy for me… being that you love your family so much… plus, you're just a pup."

"Look! I'm not going to ask again, where's my family?" she shouted. Her eyes threw daggers while her fists were clenched.

"Let's just say one foot is in this world and the other in the afterlife. Both dark and treacherous."

"What?" Kelly said, bewildered.

"Kill yourself. So that your family may live. Are you willing to do that? Otherwise, they will all die."

Kelly was speechless. She looked around, wondering if this was some kind of mind game and her family was actually okay. She wanted any hint of her family being okay. Although the house was trashed, there were no ashes anywhere. No dead witch hunters or their blood. Surely her family would have not gone down without a fight. After all, they were a very powerful master coven. That made her feel a little more hopeful. However, innocuous this man was not. She was scared for herself and, most of all, scared for her family but she remembered that her mother taught her that the worst death a person could have is to give up and take their own life. Because life is the most precious gift from God.

"Mom! Where are you?" Kelly called out.

"She can't hear you…"

Kelly continued to think, eyes welling up. She saw Thomas looking through the back window.

"Take my hand and it will all be over. Come on." He stretched his hand out toward her, closing his eyes, connecting with her essence. He smiled, liking the vibrations he got from her, feeling everything in her considering it, for the love of her family. "You've caused this family so much turmoil. I can feel it. Take my hand and you won't have to feel that guilt any longer."

Kelly was taken aback by his words. She stood there for a moment, not sure what to do. She knew deep in her heart she had caused her family so much pain, and that maybe this would make it all right. She sighed, her heart conflicting with her thoughts. Then she slowly reached her hand out to him. Her eyes fluttered, catching sight of Thomas through the window in the back of the house. He was flagging her down, shaking his head no. Thomas pointed to the forest.

Gimon saw her expression and turned around. Thomas ducked just in time. Kelly was perplexed. She had her hand still out, then slowly pulled it back.

"Do you want your whole family to die?" Gimon roared.

"No!" Kelly gave an involuntary jump.

Their eyes were locked even tighter, anger pulsing between the two of them. Kelly's mother's words about a good death played in her head. She knew she could not give up. She was determined to save her family at all costs. Gimon could see from her eyes she wasn't buying what he was selling. And it made him that much more furious.

Kelly rushed to the front door. Gimon sent a fireball, slamming the door shut. The door erupted in flames. Kelly stood frozen, stunned by his powers. He smiled as if to say *impressed?* He sent a ball of flames straight at her. Kelly stopped it with a force field that dispersed the flames all over the house. Gimon sighed, anger brewing, and released a constant stream of fire toward her. She met it with her red force field. She was in awe, wondering how he could have such an ability. They stared at each other... eyes tight as his flames pushed up against her force field, only feet in front of her. She held the constant flame at bay, feeling his power. They both used both hands, demonstrating their ultimate power.

The house shook two hard times. If it was an earthquake it would have been at least a 7.0.

Kelly looked for a place to escape but there was none. Most of the house was on fire.

Gimon stopped for a moment, frustrated by her force field. This time he threw a barrage of fireballs at her. She ducked and dodged them, blasting red shock waves back at him. He reflected them with fireballs from his hands.

The house rocked and shook from the pure force of their fighting.

Gimon then threw a green shock wave accompanied by a fireball that knocked Kelly off of her feet and onto her back. She lay dazed, trying to get her bearings. Gimon strolled up to her and stared down at her, grinning menacingly. She stared back up at him in awe, surprised that he sent a green shock wave accompanied by a fireball.

"You're a witch?" Kelly said, perplexed and in fear.

"I don't know what I am. There are so many names, hybrid witch. Hybrid witch hunter, flamer," Gimon said with an ironic smile. "So now you know my secret. Now you know why I'm so good."

Kelly stared up at him in wonderment. "Then why?" she asked. "And why do they follow you... a witch?"

"They only know what I want them to know." He snarled, "And don't call me a witch. I'm not a witch. I'm just something different."

"Well, you're not just human!"

He looked around at the spreading flames. "Like you, I'm rare. It's only a few like me. And I've only met one. So I have to be discreet. Not even my father or grandfather knew of my power. Only my mother. She explained how rare I was and that to expose my differences was to ask to be put to death. Only later I learned my mother was wrong keeping my secret, and I should have been put to death as a boy. So since I didn't have the strength to expose myself, I felt it was my duty to kill as many witches as I could find. And on my fortieth birthday, I'll finally end it for myself. That's next year. It's an agreement I made with myself when I was sixteen. So you... this little surprise... is kind of like a wonderful present for me."

Gimon stared at Kelly as if he was cursed and this was his only chance at redemption. "I like to call myself the messiah of righteousness, of all things evil."

"Are you evil?" Kelly said, hoping he would see the error of his ways. Hoping he would see that just because you don't understand something doesn't mean it's vile.

"I'm not just evil, I am the tyranny of evil men. And that's the difference between me and you. I know I'm evil and our presence on this earth is a mistake."

Kelly thinks about his words. "Well then, why would the creator make us this way?"

Gimon thought for a moment. "Because he made a mistake."

"You're the mistake, not us. Because I know my heart. And my heart is pure and good. And besides, God doesn't make mistakes."

Her words stumped him, and the sense she made only enraged him.

Kelly was worried, knowing her words cut deep and were probably the last she would ever speak.

Gimon stared at her as the smoke started to choke her. He smiled, realizing that the smoke was getting the best of her.

Kelly desperately looked around for an escape but saw no way out. Just fire.

"Maybe it's time for both of us to die," Gimon said as the flames kicked up all around them. "Embrace it, child," he said, ready to see his own maker if need be.

Kelly saw a broom by a dustpan in the corner of the room. She stared back at the man who looked down at her, ready to strike with a single flame.

Gimon's eyes showed the satisfaction of killing Kelly. "Don't fret, my child. You'll be with your family soon..."

She stared back with fear in her eyes. "What?" she exclaimed.

"Dead, in the woods... my men should be killing them this very moment. I've always had my plan B. And they'll meet you on the other side."

Kelly was devastated. She tried to throw Gimon off of her, but he was too strong. She slowed her fight, seeing her reflection in his eyes as he peered down at her.

Thomas busted the back window with a rock, making Gimon whip around... sent a shock wave that blasted the window out of the house. Thomas dove out of the way. Gimon turned back and created a fireball to throw down at

Kelly. Kelly's eyes went wide. He sent a final flame at Kelly to end this match of powers forever.

Kelly slowly pushed the approaching flame off of her. Not only were her hands red but her whole body as well. Gimon was surprised by her strength. He tried again, sending another flame. Tears streamed down Kelly's face as she pushed the flame off with all of her might, this time knocking Gimon back onto the floor. Surprised by her own power, she looked at her hands and body. Then she hopped up and ran as fast as she could to the living room window. The curtains were on fire. With a swipe of the hand she made the broom fly to her and meet her at the window just in time to jump on it as it flew through the burning curtains like a missile.

The tip of the broom pierced the burning window, shattering the glass. Part of the burning curtain wrapped itself around the broomstick, resembling a black cloak.

Mason, Cam, and Stem, who were out front, ducked as Kelly flew over their heads. They were dumbfounded, having never seen anything like that before.

Kelly flew high up in the sky, then doubled back down, flying over the Switch house toward the woods, extinguishing the burning curtain and leaving a trace of smoke in the sky.

Thomas saw Kelly flying toward the woods. He couldn't believe what he was seeing. He looked deep into the woods and could see faint flashes of purple lighting up the sky.

Gimon kicked the burning front door down. His coat was on fire. Mason, Cam, and Stem rushed to him. He gasped for the air that he desperately needed. His men tried to beat the fire off of his jacket. He pushed them away, frustrated, undaunted by the fire.

They all stared up to the sky, at the trace of smoke in the air.

"Uh, boss, that black girl just flew away," Stem said, still amazed.

Gimon looked at Stem as if he was stupid, having seen her fly out of the house and into the air himself.

"What are we going to do?" Mason asked.

Gimon looked at his men, then back at the sky bearing the trace of smoke.

"Nothing. Nothing for now. She's too powerful. And she knows it," Gimon said.

"And our men in the woods?" Cam asked.

Gimon gave him a look that said it was too late for them, and headed for his truck.

The Switch family ran through the woods, pursued by at least a couple dozen witch hunters. Their eyes said that it was all over and they were going to be defeated. The witch hunters fired on them as they ran for their lives.

Kelly flew by. The Switch family was flabbergasted, not sure what they were seeing. Kelly sent red blasts that lit up the forest, like an air strike in a war zone. The witch hunters were knocked off their feet, dazed. Kelly repeated the massive assault four more times. The Switch family watched in awe. The Woody brothers shouted, cheering Kelly on.

The witch hunters who weren't killed or severely hurt ran away, terrified of this new power.

Kelly landed beside her family. The entire family stood with mouths open in shock. The twins even looked intimidated. Linda looked at Kelly, amazed.

Kelly stared at her family, heart racing, still a little delirious and wild-eyed.

"Mom… I can fly."

Chapter 22

L inda walked up to Kelly and rubbed her cheeks, staring lovingly into her eyes.

"Mom, what should I do now?" Kelly said, heart still racing.

Linda thought about it for a moment. "Make them never, ever... want to come back," she said with a smirk.

A smile crept across Kelly's face. With a glint in her eyes, she winked at her mother. She looked at Emily and then the rest of the family. Dorothy, Carrie, Brenda, the twins, and the Woody brothers all showed nothing but love and admiration for her.

Emily ran up to Kelly and hugged her tightly. Linda stared at her girls, struggling to control her emotions. Brenda rubbed her back, knowing this was Linda's moment as a mother. Carrie smiled at Emily and Kelly, then at her own girls. Dorothy wiped a tear from the corner of her eye, taking in the only thing that's ever mattered to her— family.

"You know, you're not just my sister. You're my best friend," Emily said, proud of Kelly.

"I know. I love you too, sis," Kelly replied.

"I can't believe you saved us again!" Emily said.

"I can't believe it either," Kelly said in disbelief herself.

"The girl's on a roll," Shonda said with a chuckle.

"Well I personally am glad she is," Rhonda said.

"I guess we know what your special gift is now," Emily said, nodding at the broom in her hand.

"I guess so," Kelly said with a smirk.

"I wish I could fly," Taylor said.

"You wish you had a girlfriend," Zach said with a chuckle. They all laughed.

Emily held Kelly's hand, smiling, still in awe of her sister.

"I love you, sis," Emily said.

"I know, I know, you told me," Kelly said.

As Linda watched her daughters expressing their love for each other, Dorothy went to Linda and put her arm around her. Linda leaned into her mother, feeling the warmth of her mother's love.

"Well, go. Go fly," Linda said, using her hand to shoo her away. Everyone laughed. The Switch family couldn't help but get choked up. Even Zach and Taylor looked like they could shed a tear, but they quickly shook it off, too macho to show any emotion.

Kelly wiped the tears from the corners of her eyes. Then a hint of satisfaction showed in her expression—and she took off on her broom...

Her family watched with reverence, as she soared through the night.

As Kelly flew through the sky, she thought about how her life had come to this, and wondered what was to come in the future. She loved her family—and now extended family—more than anything. She thought about her father and how she missed him. Then she wondered about her biological mother, father, grandmother... she wondered if she had any biological brothers or sisters. She knew that her life was no longer what it once was. It would never be the same again.

Her dream of being a world-class sprinter was officially over now that she could fly. She knew it wouldn't be fair to run anymore. She smiled, amused, knowing she could literally fly to the finish line.

This was her new life and her family was all that mattered now.

She wondered if she could be with Thomas. She liked him a lot. And she knew that he liked her as well. But when it came to young love, she knew boys come and go. Trying as a teen to find a soul mate is not an easy task. Some find them, most don't. She wondered if Thomas could be the one, as she flew with the wind in her face, blowing through her hair.

Kelly felt different than she usually felt. For the first time in her life she felt uniquely herself. Like a young woman who did not have to pretend anymore. A soul who was truly the person she was meant to be. A witch. A good witch. But even as a good witch, she was going to make sure that these witch hunters were never going to mess with the Switch family ever again. She wasn't going to kill them, but she was going to make a point; if she wanted to she could.

She saw the witch hunters fleeing through the woods. She smiled and hunkered down on her broom as she approached from up above. The witch hunters down low saw her coming for them. Some of them ran faster, others hid.

Kelly's eyes narrowed as she descended like a hawk claiming its prey. She thought about when she used to run track, and how she always felt like she could just fly once she hit her stride. But never in a million years did she think she could ever fly like this.

The End

About the Author

C hristopher J. Moore holds two BA degrees, in Psychology and Film and a Master's in Screenwriting, from California State University, Northridge. His professional career began in 2000, when he won the Nickelodeon Screenwriting Fellowship. Since then, he has written for several major producers in Hollywood. He has sold screenplays and written for hit television shows, one of which ended up the highest-rated comedy series in cable television history, winning NAACP Image Awards for best TV comedy series two years in a row. He has written his First YA novel, *THE SWITCH FAMILY*, which is the first of a series, and is the author of three best-selling novels: *God's Child*, *Waiting For Mr. Right*, and *The Five Steps of Mr. Washington*.